DRAGON SHIELD

Also by Charlie Fletcher

Stoneheart
Ironhand
Silvertongue

Far Rockaway

DRAGON SHIELD

CHARLIE FLETCHER

Hodder
Children's
Books

A division of Hachette Children's Books

Text copyright © 2014 Charlie Fletcher

First published in Great Britain in 2014
by Hodder Children's Books

The rights of Charlie Fletcher to be identified as the Author of the
Work respectively have been asserted by them in accordance with
the Copyright, Designs and Patents Act 1988

1

A Catalogue record for this book is available
from the British Library

ISBN 978 1 444 91732 1

Typeset in Garamond by Avon DataSet Ltd,
Bidford-on-Avon, Warwickshire

Printed and bound in Great Britain by Clays Ltd, St Ives plc

The paper and board used in this paperback by Hodder Children's
Books are natural recyclable products made from wood grown in
sustainable forests. The manufacturing processes conform to the
environmental regulations of the country of origin.

Hodder Children's Books
a division of Hachette Children's Books
338 Euston Road, London NW1 3BH
An Hachette UK company

www.hachette.co.uk

For Dashka MacDonald

Stop/Start

The British Museum sprawls across 22 acres of London, with nearly 100 separate galleries stretching two and a half miles around it. Only a tiny fraction of the 8 million or so objects it contains are ever on display at one time. It's not just big: it's vast, and stuffed with treasures.

And secrets.

The Ancient Egyptian gallery is one of the most popular. Though it is normally full of school-trips and tourists looking at the statues, mummies and animal headed gods, today it was closed. Outside, beyond the high doors the museum was as bustling as noisy as usual, a low rumble of chatter, foot-scuffs, snatches of laughter and teachers shushing. Inside it was calmer. A group of excited museum staff crouched round a black stone coffin that looked like a clumsy bathtub with a strip of picture writing around its rim. At some stage in its long past a piece of the stone had fractured away, leaving a ragged hole that broke the flow of pictures.

The chunk of stone that had been broken off had only just come to light. The staff were there to see if it was, as they suspected, the missing piece. The museum doesn't just collect and display things. Sometimes it mends them. And on a normal day, that's a very good thing.

Maybe that's why the man in charge was smiling encouragingly at the girl who was hesitating as she held the chunk of stone up to the gap.

'Go on,' he said. 'It's not going to bite you.'

She gently fitted the piece into the gap. Completing the strip of picture writing. She didn't have time to smile back at him.

It didn't bite her. It did something much worse.

The heavy stone coffin jolted, and a blinding flash of blue light flowed around the strip of picture writing, and then everything – EVERYTHING – stopped dead.

She froze. He froze. The room froze. The museum froze. No one moved, and from the sound – or lack of it – the whole world outside came to a stop as everything was hit by a sudden and complete silence, abrupt and shocking as a hammer-blow.

On a normal day, mending things is good.

This, as noted, was not a normal day.

And sometimes things that are broken should not be fixed.

Something in the shadows moved a little. And began, quietly at first, to laugh.

It wasn't a nice laugh. And it got nastier as it got louder . . .

1

Rewind

A moment earlier, before the coffin was mended, half a mile across London, before the blue flash, Will Carter was sitting next to his sister Jo, fighting his way through a horde of mutant zombies with his thumb. The two of them were in a waiting room at the Children's Hospital, the zombies were in a game on his phone; for the first few seconds after the blue flash he thought the game had just crashed and frozen. He was already bored and angry at having to accompany his mum and Jo to the hospital in Central London, and this minor glitch felt like the last straw. He didn't like London much.

And then there was – of course – the guilt, the reason they were in the hospital again, the reason a little thing like his game glitching up felt like that last straw on an already rotten day.

Jo had a dodgy leg.

She'd got it a year ago, jumping off a wall onto a

shed roof after Will (who had just done it himself) dared her. She'd jumped just like he said he'd done, just like she always did, always trying to catch up with her brother, always trying to be a year older than she was. But the bit of roof she landed on had given way, and she fell straight through it.

It was Will's worst memory, though Jo herself couldn't recall any of it. Which was good, because it had been bad.

Like her knee now was.

It had been patched and mended as best the surgeons could manage, and she could finally walk without crutches, but she still used a stick and had to wear a special metal brace that velcroed round her leg. She had to keep coming into London, to the Kid's Hospital to have it adjusted because she was still growing.

And every time she went, their mum brought him along too. She said it was because the appointments happened in school holidays and there was no one at home to keep an eye on him because their dad was a soldier and spent most of the time abroad. Will thought it was more like she felt he had to come and be part of the hospital thing because it was all his fault. Like a punishment. Even though she said it wasn't.

And the truth is Will never refused or even complained. Not outwardly. He did sort of sulk inside though, even though he knew he had no right to feel bad about a punishment. Because even though no one else knew it, he did deserve it.

Will was a liar and a coward. He knew it, even if nobody else did. In fact he thought he was a sort of double coward. He'd lied about jumping before Jo did. He had sort of jumped onto the roof, but he'd lowered himself halfway like a normally cautious person would. Jo, who was unthinkingly brave and always trusted him, just took a running jump. So he was a coward for not actually jumping like she thought he'd jumped, and he was doubly so because he had not, could not and now would never tell her so.

In the horrible moments and hours after the roof gave way he hadn't been entirely truthful with himself because he was so shocked. He couldn't remember what he'd gabbled through the tears and panic as he tried to lift Jo back to her feet before she screamed and fainted, and then there was the horror of running for help and it all just blurred together into a fog in his head. And then afterwards no one seemed to blame him and he didn't say anything, and then he told himself it wouldn't help Jo knowing anyway, and it wouldn't change anything and so he kept quiet, thinking to himself it'd be OK to tell her later, when she was better. That was a lie he'd told himself. And then time moved on and the moment seemed to have passed and he got used to things.

He'd thought he might tell his dad when he came back off his next tour of duty, because his dad was comfortingly tough but a really good listener. But he'd come back so tired and drawn from six months in Afghanistan that Will had decided not to add to his worries, and so had kept the secret festering inside him. Their mum had said the best thing to do for his dad was to fill the house with laughter and fun, except when he needed to sleep, which he did a lot. Will missed having him around like other boys had their dads every night and at weekends. Jo had their mum, as did he, but it wasn't quite the same. So he buried it. His dad was a hero, even though he was a tired one, and having a coward for a son wouldn't have helped him much. And in truth it really wouldn't have helped Jo get better either if she'd known she'd been tricked anyway. So he was sort of keeping quiet for her. Maybe.

They'd been sitting in the waiting room for what seemed like forever. Jo had her head down over a book, which was how she avoided having to catch anyone else's eye, in case they started asking about her leg and being nice about it, which she hated. The other kids and their parents had been called in to see the doctors one by one, leaving the three of them alone in a third-floor room with seven plastic chairs and one sick looking spider plant that was dying quietly in the corner. And then their mum had told them to stay there and had gone to feed the parking meter outside, and then to maybe find a nurse to see why things were taking so long.

Jo'd grunted and carried on reading. Will was overrun by a surprise horde of zombies, and restarted the game. He'd beaten that horde and gone onto the next level with a bigger gun just before the game blipped and jammed up on his screen. He swore under his breath and was about to try and restart when she grabbed him.

'Wha—?' he began, looking up from the screen.

She didn't say anything. She was staring at the door.

'Everything stopped,' she whispered.

Her voice was dry and scratchy. Like it was a thing she didn't use much. Like her throat was rusty.

He followed her eyes and saw the flying doctor. Only he wasn't flying, he just looked like he was. Actually he was running. Or would have been, if he was moving at all. But he wasn't. He was frozen in mid-air, like a statue of a running doctor, his white coat flared out behind him, his tie streaming back over his shoulder, longish hair caught mid-bounce and sticking up like a cartoon of a mad scientist. He was leaning forward, with only the toe of his back foot touching the floor in a way that should – if the world was working right – have made him tip over and fall on his face.

Only the world wasn't working right. The doctor was suspended in mid-air, unmoving, his face caught in a grimace.

'That's not, er . . .' said Jo.

Will nodded. It wasn't.

'Where's Mum?' she said, reaching for her stick.

Will's mouth was suddenly dry and tasted metallic.

'Hang on,' he said.

It felt strange walking across the floor towards the flying doctor. At each step he expected the doctor's face to turn and see him and maybe laugh at the joke being played on them. But the doctor didn't move, and when Will got to the door and looked carefully across the corridor . . . it was worse.

Two nurses in the ward opposite were frozen like waxworks. They had been changing the sheets on a bed – one sheet was stuck mid-flip, as they snapped it out between them, billowed up like a parachute. They were smiling across it at one another. But nothing was moving at all.

He looked down the corridor. There were five people on the shiny linoleum. None of them were moving either. He wondered for an instant if this was one of those Internet pranks, where lots of people got together and did things to see what the effect on onlookers would be, filming it and posting the results on YouTube. But then he saw one of the figures was a little girl holding her father's hand and skipping in the air. Ahead of them a hospital volunteer was waiting beside a trolley with sweets and comics and magazines on it. Neither of her feet was on the ground.

It was real.

'OK . . .' said Will, swallowing as he pulled his head back inside the waiting room and turned to look at his sister. 'Everything has stopped.'

She was already right there at his shoulder, her eyes wide.

'That's not . . . possible is it?' she said.

'No,' he said.

'So I'm dreaming,' she said, a flicker of relief

11

kindling in her voice.

'No,' he said slowly. '*I'm* dreaming. And you're in my dream saying you're dreaming.'

'Will,' she said, and giggled. 'Seriously, you're in *my* dream, saying I'm in *your* dream . . .'

She suddenly pinched her arm and winced.

'Ouch.'

'What?' he said.

'I didn't wake up,' she said. 'You pinch yourself. See if you wake up!'

He pinched himself. All that happened was his arm hurt.

'I didn't wake up,' he said, looking at her.

'Maybe that's not how it works,' she said, and stepped past him, her stick clicking as she gingerly crossed the corridor into the ward with the nurses changing the sheet.

'Jo . . .' he said.

She giggled again, and beckoned him over her shoulder.

'What?' he said.

A boy was lying back on one of the beds, his mouth wide open in a huge grin, captured in the moment of upending a whole tube of Smarties into his mouth. The avalanche of sweets was frozen in a multi-coloured

12

arc that just hung in the air between the tube and his waiting face.

'Wow,' said Jo, and giggled again. She crossed to the bed and carefully swiped her hand through the flow of Smarties, grabbing a handful, leaving a gap in the flow that was as clean edged as if she'd cut through it with a knife.

'Jo . . .' said Will again.

She cupped the Smarties into her own mouth and crunched down. As she turned to look at him, her eyes were bright with glee.

'Jusht Shmarties,' she said through the mouthful of chocolate and crushed candyshell. 'Come on. Admit it. It's pretty cool, whatever it is'.

She carefully picked a red Smartie out of the air and tossed it to him. He caught it on reflex and looked down at it. He hesitated.

'Chicken,' she said.

He popped it into his mouth and bit down. Chocolate. Sugar. The usual. He grinned at her. He felt a bit light-headed.

She reached for the frozen boy's hand and pushed it. It didn't move. She pulled his wrist. It remained still.

'Hmm,' she said, and scooped more Smarties out

of the air. 'Weird. You can move *things*, but he's stuck solid.'

She walked across to the closest nurse and stuck her stick out towards her.

'Don't,' said Will.

She ignored him and pushed the nurse with the rubber tip. The nurse didn't move a bit.

'Rock solid,' she said, turning to him with a smile. 'Just like a statue.'

He noticed her eyes really were a bit too bright. Like she was determined this should be fun because if it wasn't it would be the opposite. He swallowed the last of the Smarties and looked back into the corridor full of unmoving people.

This was all so far beyond weird that he thought he might as well go with it until he woke up. He'd go with Jo's lead for a change. That way he wouldn't have to do too much thinking. It might be as fun as her eyes were trying to persuade him it was.

'There's a whole trolley full of sweets out there . . .' he said.

'Cool,' she said.

'Though that would be stealing,' he said. He should definitely just go with it; that's what you should do in a dream like this, even a dream that didn't quite feel like any dream he's ever had before.

'Not if it's all imagination,' she laughed, walking past the Smarties boy towards the window. 'Do you notice how quiet it is? Oh wow! No traffic . . . nothing's moving on the street.'

She turned and grinned at him. He really didn't like the smile. Too bright.

'Will! This could be the coolest thing ever, I mean this is a very, very, I mean, supercool dream! Forget the little sweetie trolley. It looks like we've got a whole city to play with before I wake up! No adults, all the shops open. We can do—'

'Doesn't feel like a dream,' he said, not convinced. 'Not like any dream I've ever had.'

He looked over her shoulder. The road was unnaturally still – cars and buses unmoving, pedestrians like statues, a motorbike frozen on the corner at 45 degrees to the horizontal as the dispatch rider leaned it into the turn.

'Maybe you have to pinch me,' she said. 'We should pinch each other. Pinch me first.'

'OK,' he said, and reached for her arm. Of course. That was it. You only woke up in a dream if someone else pinched you. That was it. They'd just done it wrong was all. He felt a flood of relief. And then he

15

caught a movement on the rooftops on the other side of the street and froze.

She looked at him in shock.

'Will!' she said and caught her breath.

He looked at her. She exhaled and chopped out a half-laugh.

'Don't do that! I thought you'd stopped too!'

He gripped her arm.

'Don't move,' he breathed.

When he was serious she always knew it. She went still.

'What is it?' she whispered.

'A dragon,' he said.

'Dragons don't exist,' she whispered. And even in those three short words he could hear that it already sounded more like a wish than a fact.

He pointed out of the window with a small movement of his chin.

'On the roof opposite,' he said. 'By the satellite dish.'

Jo thought she really must be dreaming, because that big thing with the silvery wings and the sharp fangs and the wet-red mouth definitely looked like a metal dragon. It was even a bit familiar: she recognized it as one of the ones that you saw on the side of the

road all round the City of London.

A statue of a dragon.

Except it was moving.

And statues shouldn't move.

It clung to the ridge of the roof with brutally curved talons, panting heavily, its sides heaving in and out as thin tendrils of dark smoke curled up from its nostrils. Its barbed tongue twitched back and forth like an angry red snake looking blindly for someone to bite. There was a kind of pent-up power to it, half wild predator coiled to spring into the attack, half dragon-shaped steam-locomotive clinging to the roof slates, about to blow. Then it turned its head, looked right back at them and roared with a power and an anger that rattled the window in its frame.

And she DEFINITELY heard that, because her guts went cold with fear and they both leaped backwards on reflex.

'See?' he said. 'Not a dream.'

'No,' she choked.

'It's a nightmare.'

2

The golden girl

They ran.

That's what you do.

A dragon looks at you and roars: you run.

It's not complicated.

The ancient bit of your brain in charge of making sure you don't end up as anything's lunch takes over and propels your body as fast as it can in the opposite direction from whatever looks remotely liable to snack on you.

They pinballed down the corridor, bumping through the unmoving people blocking their way. Will ran ahead, Jo followed in a lopsided run, half hop, half skip and occasional jump, her stick clacking with each step. They turned the corner just as they heard something smash in the waiting room behind them.

'It's trying to get in!' shouted Jo. 'Move!'

Will shouldered the swing doors that led to the

stairwell and held them open as she ducked under his arm.

She was almost as fast going down stairs as he was, using the rail as a kind of slide. They went down two flights with no problem and then she bounced off a hefty unmoving woman frozen in the act of hauling herself up the steps. She would have fallen badly had Will not snapped his arm out and caught her.

'Thanks' she gulped.

They slowed as they squeezed past the wide-hipped human roadblock, ears pricked, listening to the floors above them. It was silent. All they could hear was themselves panting for breath.

'Hear anything?' he said.

'No,' she replied.

'Maybe it wasn't chasing us?' he said, hopefully.

'Yep,' she replied, biting her lip. 'We both know this is mad, right?'

'Sure,' he nodded. 'But it's real.'

'That's the maddest bit,' she said. 'That's the worst.'

'No,' he said. 'The worst is Mum. Mum's outside.'

Jo looked at him.

'Feeding the meter. Out there with that thing.'

There was another crash and a scraping sound above them.

'No,' said Jo. 'That thing's inside. With us!'

The fear took over again and had them in motion before they knew where they were going. They helter-skeltered downwards until they passed the ground floor and only stopped when they hit an unlit landing and a door marked NO ENTRY.

It wouldn't open.

'Jo!' said Will.

He felt her hand grab his leg, then find his shoulder.

'Up one floor,' he panted. 'We're in the basement . . .'

They ran upwards again into the light and out onto the ground floor corridor. They could see the reception desk at the far end, with an unmoving wedge of people clustered around it. They got halfway towards the frozen crowd when Will stopped, halted by a glimpse of the street beyond.

'Maybe the basement's a good idea,' he said slowly. Going outside didn't seem like such a good plan after all. She cannoned into his back.

'Why?'

'Dunno. Maybe it's safe? Like a bomb shelter or something . . .'

There was a smash behind them as the doors to the stairs blew open and a ripple of gold blitzed through

21

them. For a moment Will thought it was dragon's flame, and then his eyes sort of twisted in his head to make sense of the unbelievable thing that had followed them.

It wasn't a dragon.

It was a girl.

A golden girl, like a ballet dancer made of shining yellow from the top of her head to the tip of her toes. She spun across the floor like a gilded whirlwind. She was clothed (or at least almost clothed) in a swirl of golden drapery held against her body by nothing more than a breeze that seemed to ripple around her at all times.

The golden girl looked at them. Her face shone. Her smile did something to Will's stomach, making it do a kind of hiccup.

'A boy!' she laughed in surprise. 'I *thought* I saw a boy.'

She looked at Jo.

'And a girl . . .'

She didn't sound quite so happy to see her.

'. . . a hobbling girl.'

'Who are you?' said Will.

'What are you?' said Jo.

'I am Ariel,' laughed the girl. 'I am a nimble spirit

of air and grace. I expect I am the loveliest, lightest thing you have ever seen . . .'

'You look like a statue,' said Jo.

'I am indeed a statue,' said Ariel. 'I am a very important statue. I live on top of the Bank of England, and if there is a more important roof in the city I should like to know it!'

'Palace,' said Jo. Will could tell she didn't like this Ariel. 'Buckingham Palace.'

'Palaces are for kings and queens' said Ariel dismissively. 'They come and go. Money is forever. Why aren't you two all still and lifeless like all the other people?'

She looked genuinely perplexed.

"Don't know,' said Will. 'What's happening?'

'Nothing,' laughed Ariel. 'London is full of nothing happening everywhere! I mean not to Regular people like you. No one is moving at all . . .'

She pointed down the hall at the crowd of unmoving people who filled the space like a 3D freeze-frame, some smiling, some looking worried, some looking like sleepwalkers as they were frozen mid-blink with their eyes shut, like a bad photograph.

'Everyone is still. Except you. Why is that?'

'I don't know,' said Will.

'What about the dragon?' said Jo.

'Which one?' said Ariel. 'The one that saw you upstairs, or all the other ones.'

Her smile, when aimed at Jo, was not quite nasty, but not quite nice either.

'Other ones?' said Will. He didn't like the sound of other ones. One was bad enough. 'There are other ones?'

'Oh, boy!' laughed Ariel. 'How funny you are. London is *full* of dragons. Why every important road that leads into the Square Mile at the centre is guarded by at least one dragon. Haven't you seen them? And they'll all try and grab you if they see you moving about now . . .'

'Why?' said Jo.

'What should we do?' said Will. That seemed the more important question. 'Why' could wait.

Ariel looked at them both and smiled.

'"What?" is run, "what?" is hide. "Why?" is something else entirely. "Why?" is magic. Bad magic. Something bad is happening. It is very exciting. I haven't been quite so not bored for *ages!*'

'OK,' said Jo, suddenly sounding exhausted. 'I'm out. Seriously. This is absolutely a dream, pinching or no pinching. I'm talking to a statue and it's telling me everything's magic. Wake me up when it's over.'

And she slumped down on one of the seats lining the wall and closed her eyes.

'Silly little girl,' said Ariel. 'The dragon saw you. It knows you're here. It will come for you. I came to warn you but I shouldn't have bothered, I can see.'

And as if to punctuate what she said something passed the window, blotting out the light for a moment as it did so. Ariel looked at Will.

'Go now. Run.'

'Where?' Said Will panic rising in his throat.

'Silly boy. When there's a dragon at your front door, leave by the back door. Any fool can work that out,' laughed Ariel. 'Don't try and follow me. You can't fly . . .'

And with a slow pirouette she turned and flew back the way she had come, her feet not touching the ground as she passed into the stairwell and out of sight.

'Jo,' hissed Will.

She was already on her feet.

'Back door. I heard.'

There was a scraping, thumping noise from the front door. A silver and red dragon's head rammed itself through the revolving door, but got no further as the spiny wings jammed up in the narrow gap.

Just the head and neck were bad enough: the dragon's eyes tracked furiously right and left, looking for a target, the more it tried to wedge itself through the impossible gap, the angrier it looked as it snuffled and choked with the effort. The head thrashed from side to side on the end of a long muscular neck, which made the thick red tongue flail madly back and forth between its fangs, splashing thick dragon-drool across the shiny floor, leaving gobbets hanging off the unmoving faces of the frozen people close to the exit.

Its wicked little eyes found Jo and Will, and seemed to zero in on them: Will felt like he was caught on the wrong end of a sniper's telescopic sight, trapped in the crosshairs.

Dead meat.

And then Jo's hand grabbed his collar and he was yanked through a doorway and into another long corridor.

He heard the dragon roar in frustration and was sure he felt the heat of its breath on his back as they ran.

3

Back door to a nightmare

They sprinted down the labyrinth of hallways, swerving left and right where the corners took them, but always trying to keep their bearings and head towards the back of the building.

They jinked past hospital trolleys and nurses and tea-ladies.

They sidestepped doctors and patients.

Will slipped through the narrow gap between a man stuck in the act of getting out of a wheelchair and the wheelchair itself.

Jo hopped, skipped and jumped round it.

They banged through swing door after swing door, being twisted and turned by the strange layout of the old building, always trying to keep heading away from the front.

'It's like a maze,' gasped Jo.

She was slowing down. She looked in pain. He could see her running was becoming much more jerky and lopsided. The strange thing was it made him angry with her, because now he was going to have to do something he didn't really want to, but he did it anyway, because that's what you do when your sister's hurt and it might be your fault even though it obviously isn't.

'Wait,' he said, and spun round, running back the way they'd just come.

'Will!!!' she shouted. 'You're nuts! Where are you going?!'

She stood staring back at the swinging door, and then heard ominous banging as something came back towards her at speed. The door flew open to reveal Will pushing the wheelchair.

'Turn round!' he yelled. She did, just as he reached her, dropping into the seat almost without him having to stop. She stuck her good leg out in front of her, and they booted through the next two sets of doors without stopping, using it like a battering ram.

Then suddenly there was nothing in front of them but a blank door with EMERGENCY EXIT written across it.

'This is definitely an emergency!' said Will, heading straight for it.

Jo kicked the release bar as they hit it. The door

clunked open, and then they were out in the sunlight bumping down a short flight of concrete steps into the street beyond.

Jo yelped and gripped the armrests to stop flying off, while Will threw himself backwards and tried to stop their forward progress with his bodyweight. He leaned too far back though, and as they hit the pavement he managed to tip the whole chair back on himself. The sharp edge of the last step whacked him in the kidneys, and he lay there trying to get his breath, winded by the impact.

'You OK?' said Jo, craning round.

'No,' he gasped. Of course he wasn't OK. He was hurting and she was squashing him, her and the chair.

'Me neither,' she said. 'But at least we're out of there.'

She scrabbled to her feet and pulled the chair off Will.

'Seriously,' she said. 'We should get as far from here as we can. As fast as we can'

He unfolded back onto his feet.

'Ouch,' he said.

'Shhh . . .' she replied, holding her finger to her lips and looking round.

'What?' he whispered. 'What can you hear?'

'Nothing,' she said. 'That's what's so creepy.'

He listened. The city was silent. And that was definitely very creepy. London is never silent. There was no background growl of traffic. No street noise, no sirens in the distance, no slap of feet on the pavements, no laughing, no talking, no anything.

Just a blanket of silence, the kind of silence you get in the middle of the night after a heavy snow fall. The world was . . .

'Asleep,' said Jo. 'It's like the world has just . . . gone to sleep.'

'We're not dreaming,' Will said. It was so real and yet so creepily un-real that he wished they were.

'No,' she agreed. 'It all hurts too much. Much worse than pinching. If we were dreaming I'd definitely have woken up by now.'

The road in front of them was a back street with just a van on it. A motorcycle dispatch rider had pulled his bike onto the pavement and was frozen in the act of taking a package out of the box on the back of his bike. His helmet was balanced on the seat. Will picked it up. It was easier to do something, to keep moving than it was to just sit there and think about what a weird place they found themselves in.

'What are you doing?' said Jo.

'Put it on, get back in the chair,' said Will. 'We're going to go fast. Like you said.'

Jo looked at him for a beat, then nodded, put the helmet on and sat back on the chair. Will got behind it and started to push, slow at first, then faster and faster, until he got up to running speed.

'Where are we going?' shouted Jo, her voice muffled by the visor on the helmet.

'Find Mum,' he said. 'Where she put the car. By that park.'

As he ran he tried to get his bearings. They had left the car by a park called Coram's Fields. It was a short walk from the hospital and he knew its name because they used to have their sandwiches there and Mum had told them the story of the park and why it was for kids and their parents or guardians – but no one else. It was the only park you couldn't go into without a kid. Coram had been a rich man who'd left all his money to orphans a long time ago. Mum liked old stories and told them all about it the first time they went there.

That first time they'd come to one of these appointments she had tried to dress it up like a treat: they'd gone to a museum in the morning, done some

31

sightseeing and after the appointment they'd been to see a musical at the theatre. Will hadn't found the museum very interesting and it was too full of other kids on school-trips to really see anything, and going to see a musical was more for Jo than him.

The bit he'd enjoyed most had been rummaging through an antique shop close to the museum that had a lot of swords and spears and things, but he had not been allowed to touch them, let alone buy one. All they'd been able to afford was three old beads that Jo had chosen from a bowl full of random things. They looked like little coffee beans, but the shop owner, who looked almost as bored as Will had felt, said they were ancient beads.

'Ancient beads made in China last month,' his friend Jack had said when he saw it. 'Ancient people didn't have coffee anyway.'

The bead did look like a sort of coffee bean, though the man in the shop had said it was an Ancient Egyptian sacred beetle, a scarab. Will had it on a friendship bracelet that Jo had plaited when they got home. She wore the matching one. Her mum had the third bead, but she had it on her key ring instead. Jo said it was for luck, so he had not taken it off for nearly a year. It was meant to fall off naturally. He'd got used to it. Secretly he hoped that when it fell off he might stop feeling angry and guilty about being a coward and a liar. He looked down at Jo's hand gripping the arm of the chair: her bead was almost invisible, hidden in a whole bunch of bracelets jiggling on her wrist as the wheels bounced across the uneven paving stones.

He ran up a residential street with old brick Georgian houses on one side and a concrete and glass council estate on the other. He nearly tipped the chair over again as he had to clump it off the kerb into the street to avoid a crocodile of primary school kids road-blocking the pavement. Jo just held on without a squeak of protest, and he kept going, even though his arms and legs were beginning to burn with the effort.

Jo looked at the kids as he pushed her past them: they looked normal, red-cheeked, bright-eyed, just like what they were – people. The only difference was that they weren't moving. On reflex Jo put her hand out to touch one as they passed.

'What are you doing?' shouted Will.

Her hand smacked into the teacher's arm. From the brief moment of contact Jo could feel that she was warm, and soft, just as if she was normal and alive but her body was also, strangely, as unmoving as a slab of stone. Their forward momentum wrenched Jo's arm painfully backwards.

'Ouch,' she grunted.

'Stop mucking about!' said Will breathlessly. 'Or you'll have us both over.'

He turned a corner and then another, and then there it was: Coram's Fields – one of those sudden open green spaces that London hides in the tangle of its streets. It was surrounded by railings and dotted with huge old trees with thick nubbled trunks that disappeared into bushy explosions of leaves that overhung the grassy space beneath. And there they saw their car, like an old friend parked opposite.

And even better, between them and it, frozen in motion as she jogged across the street towards them was the familiar figure of their mother, disconcerting in its stillness, her coat whipped backwards, her wallet still open in her hand.

Jo got out of the chair as they approached and tugged at her mother's sleeve. She didn't react. Her brow was furrowed and she looked worried. The lack of life in the familiar face was horrible.

They stared at her.

'It's like she's, you know . . .' said Jo.

She didn't need to finish. Will could see it.

34

'She looks like she's just about to move again,' he said. 'Any minute . . .'

Jo suddenly hugged her and kept tight hold.

'No,' she choked, her voice muffled in the folds of her mother's coat. 'She looks like dead people must look.'

Will didn't know what to do. He stared round the street, full of still cars and people like statues. No one was looking. There were no dragons on the rooftops. It was like the still world was a true picture and Jo and he were the mistake, the only moving things in it. He felt a nasty lurch of aloneness. He put his arms round his mother and Jo and squeezed.

'She's still warm,' he said. His voice sounded rough. He cleared his throat. 'She's soft and warm. Like always. Not like she's dead.'

Jo pulled at her. She didn't move a bit.

'Can't move her,' she said. 'We can't leave her here. If things start moving she might get hit by a car. She's in the middle of the road . . .'

Will tugged at her, but there was no doubt. She wouldn't move. He looked round at the cars on the street. Their mother was clearly jinking her way through the traffic in her hurry to get back to them. It didn't look like she was about to get hit, and she was usually quite nimble. But she did seem very exposed. He tried, as he often did, to think what his dad would do. He wouldn't just stand around wondering; he was always moving, always doing something.

Will pulled the wallet from between her fingers and snapped it shut. Jo looked at him.

'Anyone could come along and nick it,' he said, feeling a bit silly. She took it from his hand and slid it into her mother's pocket.

'I don't think anyone else is moving except us,' she said. 'I'm scared.'

'Yeah?' he asked. Her chin came up in a defiant way he knew only too well. He grinned, though he didn't feel like smiling at all. 'Yeah. Well. I bet I'm more scared than you are.'

She tried to smile back at him but didn't quite manage to.

They were both too busy trying to be brave for each other that they didn't hear the creak in the tall tree across the road in the park.

They didn't see the angry silvered eyes peering through the thin canopy of leaves at them. They didn't see the metal talons gripping the tree, scarring the bark as they squeezed in anticipation. They didn't see the dragon at all.

But it saw them.
It was watching them.
Waiting to jump.

4

She-who-is-powerful

There was another place in London where there were sounds, another building in which there was movement. But what was moving through its galleries was not human, nor was it made of flesh and blood.

Deep in the endless rooms of the British Museum a large dog was growling, making a deep, almost sub-sonic rumble. Anyone walking through the museum would have read the label on the wall behind him and believed that his name was 'Molossian Hound'.

Not that anyone one was walking through the museum. All the people under its roof were as unmoving as most of the statues and exhibits they had come to see.

His name was not Molossian Hound. That's just what the museum called him. He knew his real name, though no one living now did. His name was Filax. He knew this because that is what the sculptor who spent months of his life freeing him from the block

38

of Italian stone in which his shape had been hidden had called him as he chipped patiently away with his chisel.

True artists and craftsmen put something of themselves into everything they make, and the man who made Filax was the truest of artists. He set out to make a deep-chested guard dog with a rough mane of hair around his neck and shoulders, and that is what he produced, but more than that he was a man who loved dogs for their great hearts and their loyal friendship, and so he made a dog that had an inner spirit that was both staunch and playful.

Filax had one other characteristic of real dogs. He had the ancient, unthinking hatred of cats. And that was why the hair on his back was standing on end, and why his lip was curling back, revealing his powerful teeth.

There were cats prowling the galleries, and they were getting close to him. He could sense them. He could smell them. He could see a strange blue light moving closer, sending shadows scuttling across the walls. And above all, he could hear them talking.

'Dog,' said a voice, a scratchy voice, half hiss, half yowl. 'Careful sisters. There is a disgusting dog in the dark.'

The ancient, unthinking hatred works both ways.

The movement stopped. Filax listened to the sound of the silence listening right back at him.

He rumbled another warning, deep in his chest.

'He is growling,' said a new voice, much like the first.

Filax lowered his head, ready to spring at whatever was about to turn the corner and enter his space.

But what he saw was not a cat. It was a woman's legs, a woman made of black stone that both shone and sucked in light. And then the legs of three more stone women walked in and stood around him in a half circle.

Filax smelled cat, more cat than he had ever smelled in one place, but the human bodies confused him. And then he looked up and saw there was something wrong with their faces.

It was hard to see exactly, because their eyes blazed a blue light that dazzled him, but he could tell they were not human heads. They were the faces of lionesses, and their great cat-heads wore Egyptian headdresses that fanned out behind them like cobra hoods. The hoods matched the single small snakehead that topped off each headdress, vicious mini cobras that sat above their brows moving from side to side, hissing as they did so.

The cat-women looked at him.

Filax growled.

The lion-women didn't move. One of them laughed.

'Bad dog,' she purred.

'Careful sister' said another, reaching out and gripping her arm. The first one shrugged off her grip.

'He is made of stone,' she snarled. 'Everything made of stone can be made to obey us now. We have awoken. Our power has returned'

Another one nodded and stepped closer. She had a stick in her hand.

'He will obey,' she said, and hefted the stick. Filax could see she was preparing to beat him. He could hear the happy anticipation in her voice.

'Not us,' said the cautious one. 'Not this one. Not even though he is made of stone. He cannot obey us. He is dog.'

'He is dog,' agreed the fourth. 'He is filth.'

'Bad dog,' said the first, turning to the cautious one. 'What would you have us do then, sister?'

'Chase the dog,' she answered, fast and vicious. 'Hurt the dog.'

'Hurt the dog before it hurts us,' agreed the one with the stick.

'Hurt the dog!' they all snarled.

The stick moved so fast the dog had no time to dodge it. It smacked into the side of his head and sent him sprawling back into the corner of the wall. The lion-women moved in.

The stick whipped back for another blow, almost fast as sight.

Filax was not made to be beaten. He was not made to be scared. He was made to protect. And he knew that these creatures meant him harm, and so the first thing he had to protect was himself.

He came out of the corner low and hard. He didn't look for a gap in the wall of stone legs blocking his escape route. He hit them like a rocket and made his own hole. He heard the stick whistling through the air as he passed and felt the pain of it biting into his side.

He spun on his heels and snapped his jaws on it, gripping hard and then twisting round on himself as he sprung back towards the exit to the gallery.

The lion-women were snarling and falling over themselves to get at him, but the power in his shoulders yanked the stick-holder off her feet, and the other two tripped over her tumbling body.

Filax ran for the door, dragging his attacker behind

him. She did not let go of the stick until her head hit the edge of the archway as he ran through it. There was a crunching noise, and then he had the stick and no attacker, so he spat the weapon out and ran for the big space at the centre of the museum, a huge courtyard covered by a glass dome, at the centre of which stood a cylindrical stone building with wide stairs rising on both sides.

Without thinking he bounded up them, taking five steps at a time.

Behind him he could hear a howling and the smack of feet on stone as the lion-women ran after him.

He was almost all the way up the stairs before the first of them burst into the Great Court behind him. He reached the top landing and turned, ready to throw them back down the stairs if they followed him.

But they didn't.

'STOP!'

A great voice boomed round the courtyard. It was a deep woman's voice.

The four women with the lioness heads stopped as one, as if yanked by an invisible string.

They turned in on each other. The voice did not come from any of them. It seemed to come from everywhere. It was almost as if it was all their voices, speaking as one.

'NO TIME FOR SPORT!' the voice roared. 'DOG HUNTING CAN COME LATER.'

The four nodded. A small cat emerged from the shadows and walked amongst their legs, sinuously rubbing itself on them. They paid it no attention, staring in hatred up the steps towards their prey, who growled back at them.

'What has happened?' said the one who had now regained her stick.

'THE DRAGONS ARE HUNTING,' said the voice.

There was a flutter from the dark door to the gallery beyond the lion-women, and a large stone hawk flapped out and landed between them. Its head flicked from one to the other, its eye a perfect white circle with a large dark centre. The jerky movements of its head and the fact that the eye did not ever blink gave it a mad look, as if it was trying to figure out from which of these four figures the everywhere-voice was coming.

'The dragons guard the city . . .' said the cautious lion-woman. The other three looked at her, the blue light blazing from their eyes casting giant shadows against the pale stone-clad walls of the courtyard.

'THE DRAGONS WORK OUR WILL' said the

everywhere-voice. 'WE CHOSE THEM FIRST BECAUSE THEY GUARD THE CITY. WHO WOULD CONQUER A CITY SHOULD FIRST CONTROL THOSE WHO GUARD IT. THIS STRANGE COLD CITY HAS DRAGON GUARDS. WE TOOK THEM. THEY BECAME US. WHO FLEES A DRAGON WORKS AGAINST US. WE WILL NOT ALLOW ENEMIES TO SURVIVE.'

'Who is the enemy?' said the cautious one.

'WE WILL SEE,' said the voice. 'HORUS THE HAWK WILL BE OUR EYES!'

There was a flash, and then the stone hawk's white eye glowed blue, the beam cutting into the gathering gloom like a searchlight.

'GO,' said the voice.

The hawk flapped its wings and clawed its way into the air, picking up speed as it climbed. It spiralled once round the great central building and then hit one of the triangular panels that made up the dome. Stone hit glass, and glass lost, smashing into glittering shrapnel that splashed and tinkled to the paving stones below, so that for an instant the four lioness headed women and the small cat twining between their legs were caught in a glass shower that bounced off them without any harm.

As one their eyes looked up, the beams of blue light meeting at the new hole in the roof, just for a moment making the outline of a pyramid.

'FEAR US ALL WHO HEAR,' said the everywhere-voice. 'WE ARE SHE WHO IS POWERFUL. WE ARE THE CLAWS OF BAST THE MIGHTY HUNTRESS. TOO LONG HAVE WE BEEN PENNED IN STONE. NOW WE WALK AMONGST YOU AGAIN. ALL SHALL OBEY AND THOSE WHO CAN NOT WILL BE DESTROYED, FOR WE ARE ALSO SEKHMET, THE FIERY EYE OF DESTRUCTION. PRAY WE DO NOT LOOK UPON YOU!'

The little cat stepped between them and also looked up, just for a moment, before looking away with a feline shrug of disinterest and padding off towards the curving stairs at the centre of the courtyard.

At the top of the stairs, hidden by the curve of the building, Filax felt the hairs on his neck rise again, but this time he killed the growl in his throat before it escaped. Filax the fearless heard the words of the everywhere-voice, and for the first time in his long existence felt something new: Filax the fearless felt frightened.

5

The Dragon's Shield

Will and Jo both tried pulling at their mother, but though she was soft and warm as ever, she was also as immoveable as if she had iron roots anchoring her to the spot.

They couldn't budge her at all.

They didn't talk as they tugged at her, but they kept catching each other's eyes across her unmoving body, and each could see how uncomfortable this was making the other.

'Do you think she can see and feel what we're doing?' said Jo. 'Do you think she's like those paralyzed people who can take everything in but not move?'

'No' said Will. 'I don't think she's working at all. I think everyone is frozen like in a freeze-frame in a video or something. There's no pulse.'

Jo nodded. Her eyes were wet.

'Where—?' she began.

She didn't finish. Because at that moment the top

of the tree in the park cracked and splintered as the dragon launched forward and erupted from the canopy in an explosion of leaves and twigs.

They spun, horrified, and saw it slam onto the tarmac in front of them with a monstrous impact that sounded like a garbage truck dropping out of the sky.

It was an ugly dragon.

Its brow overhung hot, angry little eyes.

It might have been the same dragon from the hospital. Its mouth made the same cruel curves around its fangs, and the red-painted tongue that flopped back and forth like a wet, barbed snake with a mind of its own was familiar.

It clanged its heavy metal shield on the ground, then shook it angrily at them.

'It's trying to scare us,' said Will.

'It's doing a pretty good job,' said Jo, her voice shaky. 'We should run—'

'Where to?' said Will. 'It would get us before we got five paces.'

'Got a better plan, then?' said Jo.

'Talk to it?' he said.

'You're mad,' she said. There was a short beat of silence. 'Mind you, so's all of this . . .'

They looked at each other. She shrugged. Her face looked pinched and tight with fear.

'Might as well give it a go.'

He swallowed. Just because it was his idea didn't mean it was a good one. How do you talk to a dragon, really? It wasn't something they'd covered in school.

He raised his hand, palm up. Trying not to let the wash of dread in his guts wobble it too much.

'Er . . .' he said.

'Brilliant . . .' said Jo under her breath.

She could be really annoying.

'Er . . . hi,' he said.

The dragon cocked his head, like a dog.

'. . . but go on,' said Jo. 'I think he's listening.'

'Listening's good,' said Will. 'Right?'

'Well,' she hissed, 'It's better than the alternative. Keep going!'

Will tried not to think of what the alternative might be, but the more he tried not to think of it the more words like 'eating' or 'slashing' or 'burned to a painful crisp' kept rushing into his head.

'We didn't mean to upset you,' he said. And then cleared his throat. 'I mean if we did. If that's why you're angry . . . ? It was a mistake . . .'

'You can't talk to it, boy. It just hates you.'

51

The voice came from behind him. He turned to see Ariel floating there. She didn't look at him. Her eyes were on the dragon.

'Why does it hate us?' he said.

'It's a Taint,' she said. As if that explained anything.

'What's that?' he said.

'Our word for a statue that isn't human. They hate humans, and they hate us.'

'Us?' said Jo. Ariel looked at her and shook her head as if talking to a very dim child.

'Spits,' she said.

'Spits?' said Will, watching the dragon again. It was gulping in air, and its throat was beginning to swell. Not good, he thought.

'Spits are statues that are made to be like you,' said Ariel. 'To look like the spitting image of regular humans . . .'

'Why do they hate . . .' began Jo.

Ariel gave a short snort.

'Do you think now is quite the time for a lesson, silly little girl?'

Jo looked at the dragon.

'No,' she gulped.

'No indeed,' said Ariel. 'This time, when I say run, run and don't stop until you get out of the city.'

Will could see she was tensing her muscles and bunching her fists, ready to move.

'Why are you helping us?' he said.

She snorted again.

'Oh, I'm not helping you because you're anything special, boy,' she said, laughing lightly. 'Don't flatter yourself. I'm "helping" you because she's a Taint and I'm a Spit, and I like them as little as she likes me. Like cats and dogs. And she wants you, so it's my pleasure to make sure she doesn't get what she wants . . .'

'And you're going to fight her just because.'

She flashed him a quick look that was sharp as an axe.

'I told you to run. I'm not going to *fight* dragons for you.'

'Then what are you going to do?' said Will.

The Dragon was gulping in air in great whooping breaths now, and its neck was swelling like a bird's crop. He noticed that it was beginning to glow, as if there was fire kindling inside it. He was, he realized, too scared to run, because if he turned his back he was sure the dragon would leap on him.

'Oh I'll just distract it,' sighed Ariel. 'Dragons are easy to distract. Especially with gold . . .'

She looked down at herself.

'And why, I'm practically made out of gold. They get strange feelings when I'm around. Sometimes, at night when I'm spotlit on my roof I look down and see them looking up at me. I look very fine, and they look very . . . covetous. Like they want to possess me. Nothing a dragon likes more than a hoard, and nothing looks better in a hoard than gold. And to tell the plain truth nothing looks better in gold than me. Now look out and run—'

And before he could say anything she had pushed him aside and flown straight at the dragon.

The dragon wasn't expecting that. Its little eyes widened, it made a strangled choking sound – coughing out a black smoke ring – and then, at the last moment, it ducked.

Ariel flew in low over the lip of the shield, over its ducking head, straight through the centre of the smoke ring. She reached her hand down, grabbing its tail as she went. The dragon squawked in surprise, face-planting on the pavement and dropping its shield as she yanked it and flew straight upwards, pulling its tail after her.

She wasn't strong enough to keep hold for long, but she did manage to keep a grip as she climbed about thirty feet into the air. It swung beneath her like a very angry pendulum, trying to twist back on itself and get its fangs into her arm. She laughed and let go as it reached the very end of its arc, swinging it away from Will and Jo, throwing it back into the park beyond the railings. It was tumbling upside down, and there was not enough room between Ariel's hand and the rapidly approaching ground for it to right itself and get its wings sorted out before it bounced on the turf, leaving a gouge as it tumbled backwards into a wide and bulbous tree trunk.

Will turned and shouted at his sister.

'Run!'

Jo ran in front of their mother and tugged at her, trying desperately to drag her to safety.

Maybe because she didn't just save herself, maybe because she thought first about their mother, maybe that explained what Will did next.

Maybe that's why he too did not just run away in panic. Or maybe not. He himself never remembered why he did it, only that it felt like the right thing to do.

Perhaps he had worked out that even with both of them pushing there was no way they could get to safety before the dragon came after them. Perhaps that was why he knew they needed some extra protection they could take with them.

Perhaps that was why he ran forward and picked up the dragon's shield.

Maybe he thought it could save them.

But no maybes explained how he lifted it. It was a big heavy thing, and in the normal course of events he couldn't have begun to pick it up.

Maybe because the day was already so far away from anything like the normal course of anything, the usual rules didn't apply.

Maybe.

Whatever the reason, he ran forward and flipped the shield, grabbing the strap on the back of it, and held it on his arm.

Whatever the maybes of going back for the shield, the moment he had it he knew it was definitely a mistake.

The dragon charged, and now it didn't have to hold the shield it bounded forward using all four limbs, the front talons ripping into the ground and hurling itself forward, then the powerful back legs kicking in like steam pistons as it sprang towards him.

He heard a cry from behind him and a clatter and turned, catching a quick glimpse of his sister and mother – Jo had hit the curb and toppled the wheelchair, catching her mother and cradling her head as she fell.

There was no way they would get away from the dragon now.

Ahead of him there was a metallic clang as the dragon leapt up onto the high park railings and stood there, cocking its head back on its long snake neck, like a cobra about to strike.

Only Will could see, from the smoke beginning to escape from its nostrils and the red metallic glow building in its chest, that it was about to flame them.

He scrambled back, dragging the shield with him and fell in front of the wheelchair.

'Get behind me!' he shouted, just as the Dragon spat wildfire.

He lifted the shield and caught the twisting rope of flame on the centre of the red cross painted on its front.

The wildfire had a punch like the jet from a power-hose. The impact knocked Will backwards a metre, but he braced himself and kept the metal between him and the dragon. The shield juddered in his grip, and he saw the wildfire deflected off it at an angle.

It hit a rubbish bin and ignited it.

The dragon took a deep whooping breath and then shrieked a second jet at him.

Seeing the burning bin gave him an idea. He bunched his muscles and caught the jet on the shield. The shield was becoming uncomfortably hot, but he knew if he dropped it, it would be the end. So he concentrated all his strength in turning the ricocheting wildfire back across the pavement from the flaming bin, across the park railing, where it ignited the bushes beyond, and then, slowly around it higher and higher until he was reflecting the flame straight back at the dragon itself. The wildfire hit the dragon's talon where it was gripping the metal railing.

There was no reaction at first.

Then the foot got red hot, then very quickly white hot as the wildfire twisted round it, climbing the dragon's body and wrapping it in tendrils of flame that moved as if they had a mind of their own. The fire spread along the sharp railings too.

The dragon shrieked in anger and then pain, and choked off the hose of flame.

And for a long moment it looked at Will. Then it looked at the fire still twisting round its torso and stretching like a creeper along the railings. And then it shrieked again as it tried to leap at Will and Jo.

Its wings flared and its talons reached for them, but it only fell forward.

It snarled in frustration. Its stubby wings thrashed the air as it threw itself upwards, straining to fly, and for a moment it did look as if it was about to break free, and then it fell back with a shocked squawk and a sound of metal on metal.

It fell heavily onto the spikes along the top of the fence, red hot flaming spikes that pierced its body like hot nails sliding through a pat of butter.

'Wow,' breathed Jo.

The Dragon flopped and pulled at the railings that were now sticking out of its other side, but it couldn't free itself.

'Dragon kebab,' said Will. He started to laugh, short gouts of laughter that were not like real laughing, that were unnatural to his own ears. He knew it must be hysteria and relief.

Something golden and angry landed between him and the struggling dragon.

Ariel.

'Why aren't you running?' She said. She sounded angry. 'I told you to run.

'I defeated it!' he said, pointing at the impaled dragon. 'It's done! Kebabbed!'

He had never felt such elation. Such great pride. Such a huge relief. Such . . . power.

'It's not done!' she snarled.

And at that moment the dragon snapped its neck like a whip and fired a power hose jet of flame right at them.

Ariel spun and caught the fire in the centre of her torso. She staggered back and then made herself step forward into the blast.

Protecting Will and Jo and their mother.

Blocking the flameburst.

She screamed right back at the dragon, not a scream of fear or pain, or maybe not just those things, but mainly a scream of pure defiance.

The noise hit the dragon like a solid punch of air, slamming its head sideways. The fire guttered out and the head dropped, the chin clunking onto the paving stones, the last fire dying in the angry little eye that glared at them and then went out.

'*Now* it's done . . .' whispered Ariel.

And she dropped to one knee.

And then she folded in on herself in an impossible move.

She bent as if her spine was hinged where it shouldn't be, twisting towards them as she fell.

They saw with horror that she was melted by the force of the dragonfire. Her face was lopsided. She tried to smile. Will felt a terrible stab of guilt at her bravery.

'And so am I . . .' she breathed, just about managing the smile she was reaching for before she slumped forward, her chin dropping into her chest and staying there.

For a moment the city was silent again and all Will could hear was the sound of the blood in his ears.

The dragon's shield suddenly felt like lead on his arm.

He dropped it with a clang.

'Will,' said Jo.

'She's dead,' he said, his voice strangely thick. 'It's OK. We're safe. But she's dead. It's my fault. We should have run.'

Of course it was his fault. Ever since Jo's accident everything was his fault. In fact they wouldn't even be in London if it hadn't been for the hospital appointment and that was definitely down to him. He felt the familiar wash of self-disgust begin to fill the void in his guts. He raised his eyes and looked at Jo.

Jo wasn't looking at him. She was looking into the sky, face white with terror. She pointed at a dark winged shape coming in low over the rooftops towards them.

'There's something coming. Some kind of bird. A hawk maybe?'

6

The Finsbury Angel

It wasn't a hawk, or a dragon. Jo and Will squinted into the air at the dark shape winging towards them through the late afternoon gloom. True, the black thunderclouds massing behind it gave whatever it was a doomy end-of-the-world feeling, but whatever it was, it definitely wasn't a dragon.

Dragons don't – as a rule – wear long billowy dresses.

'It's an angel . . .' said Will. 'Well. I think it's an angel, anyway . . .'

'Should we run?' said Jo, her eyes fixed on the incoming figure. Now it was closer they could hear the deliberate, unhurried sound of its wing beats like slow whip-cracks lashing in at them from above.

'Angels are the good guys, right?' said Will uneasily. 'We shouldn't be scared of angels.'

He didn't sound too convincing, even to himself.

'So why have you picked up the shield?' said Jo. He

looked down at this arm. He hadn't realized he'd done so.

'Dunno,' he said. He squinted at the approaching figure. Something had shifted, making it look suddenly monstrous.

'Angels don't have two heads,' Jo gasped. 'Let's run—'

As it got closer they saw, with horror, that it did appear to have a second head sticking up from its right shoulder.

'Stay,' said the angel. The voice sounded as though it was right next to each of them, whispering low and calm in their ears even though it was 500 metres away. It had a power that soothed and stopped – for the moment – the immediate urge to sprint away. 'Stay for a moment. Have no fear of us . . .'

'Yeah!' piped a chirpy voice that came from the second head. 'Hold up! We ain't villains. We're nice as pie, we are!'

'She's giving someone a piggyback,' said Jo, relaxing a fraction.

Closer still they could see the second head was not attached to the angel but was indeed the grinning brown face of a bronze child who was holding onto the angel's neck with one arm while waving enthusiastically with the other.

'It's a kid,' said Jo.

'Angels don't give piggybacks,' said Will, hefting the comfortable weight of the shield on his arm. 'I mean that's not exactly normal, is it?'

'No,' said the woman's voice. 'None of this is normal. There is much to fear. But none of it from me. I will not harm you. I do no harm to those who mean well. I only harm those who would do hurt to us.'

'Yeah. Well I just broke a dragon,' he whispered to Jo.

They watched her flap lazily in to land, wings folding neatly back the moment her bare feet touched the ground. As soon as that happened the bronze boy leaped to the ground and turned a somersault, bouncing to his feet throwing his arms wide with a loud smiling 'Ta da!' as if he was a circus acrobat performing a trick.

In one hand he held what looked like a mask. He was bare chested and bare legged and his uncombed hair stuck up in all directions, making him look like the most roguish street urchin imaginable.

'Calm down, Tragedy,' said the angel. 'You will frighten them.'

He tutted and slumped his shoulders, lifting the

65

mask to his face: it was a grotesque, sad expression, and was a complete contrast to his actual face which was all smiles and mischief.

The Angel was slightly larger than normal sized, but not enough to be freakish, and did not break step as she continued walking towards them. Though she was clearly made from heavy bronze and was darkened with time to a mottled grey-green colour, streaked with what can only have been pigeon droppings, she stepped lightly. The boy was also made of bronze, but his was shiny and deep brown, as if he lived indoors and was frequently polished. Her hair was held back in a band across her forehead, and her garment was, Will noted, about as wispy as Ariel's had been.

The boy dropped the mask and stuck his right hand out.

'Wotcher!' he said. 'I'm Little Tragedy, though my mates call me Tradge. Who are you?'

Will took his hand gingerly, and then flinched as the boy pumped it up and down enthusiastically.

'I'm Will. This is Jo.'

'Cor. She's a pippin,' winked Tradge. Jo didn't take his hand, just sketched a slightly stunned wave at him, whilst exchanging a questioning look at her brother.

Little Tragedy took no offence because his attention was taken by the angel who had calmly walked past them and was examining the melted and broken golden figure behind them.

'Blimey,' he said. 'What you done to my mate Ariel?'

'The Dragon did it,' said Will, and immediately felt guilty as the angel looked up and caught his eye with a steady look. That wasn't the truth of it. 'But it was my fault really. At least . . . she was hurt because of me.'

'Because of us,' said Jo.

That was his sister. Always trying to do what he was doing, even if it meant sharing the blame for stuff she hadn't done. Even in the middle of all this craziness it annoyed him. Maybe *because* of all the craziness: being angry with Jo, and then feeling complicated and bad about that too was, at least, familiar and comforting. And nothing else about right now was *close* to familiar. Nothing was comforting, certainly not the over-friendly bronze urchin whose tousled hair, he had just noticed, disguised a couple of small nubby horns, like a faun he'd once seen in a book about mythology. Even this angel was unsettling.

She walked past them and looked at Ariel. Without

saying anything she walked on and touched the unmoving dragon impaled on the railings.

'Victory,' she said, turning to look at them.

'Sorry?' said Will.

'I'm not an angel,' she said. 'I am Victory. The Finsbury Victory, to be exact.'

'Sorry?' said Jo, looking at Will.

''Er plinth is up Finsbury way in Spa Green Gardens,' said Little Tragedy.

'But don't apologise,' said Victory, 'people often mistake us Victories for angels.'

'Us?' said Will.

'Lots of Winged Victory statues in London,' she said.

'You Regulars fight a lot of wars,' said Little Tragedy. 'Always on for a dust-up or a big bit of argey-bargey.'

'Regulars?' said Jo.

'Regular people who ain't statues,' said Little Tragedy. 'You know, you lot who think we don't move too: Regulars. No offence.'

'Little Tragedy is normally on the ceiling of a pub . . .' Victory began.

'The Black Friar,' said Little Tragedy proudly. 'Most magnificent pub in the whole bloomin' city.'

'So everyone he sees is a regular to him' smiled Victory. 'Only they're all adults. That's why he comes out to find the other statues of children to find someone to play with. I was giving him a lift.'

'I was looking for Ariel,' he explained, looking a the bent body with a pantomime grimace. 'She's good for a laugh, normally. Likes a jape. Never seen her look like that before though.'

'Was she a Victory?' asked Will, guiltily nodding at Ariel's unmoving shape.

'No,' laughed Victory. Will was surprised at how lightly she was taking the destruction of the other statue. 'She's just Ariel. "A Spirit of the Air". And a very vain and conceited one at that. She's a bit of a brat . . . and sometimes so willful that I doubt she's all Spit.'

'She told us about Spits and Taints but I don't get it,' said Jo. 'Mind you I wish I wasn't getting any of this, to tell you the truth . . .'

'Not much to get,' said Tragedy. 'If it looks human, it's probably a good 'un, if it looks like a monster, a gargoyle or one of them scaly dragon bleeders – run like 'ell. Spits is good, Taints ain't. End of.'

'The dragon's a Taint?'

'Dragon's a dead Taint. For now. And Taints hate

Spits, always have, always will, because they don't have a spirit inside them like we do, they have a hole instead where it should be, so they're always hungry, always angry and always in a bad bleedin' temper.'

Will knew how they felt. But he didn't say that.

'And they normally fight like this?' he said instead.

'No.' said Victory. 'None of this is normal. Normally we just get along in a kind of truce. We give each other a wide berth. And you Regulars never see us, because you know statues that move are impossible, and your minds don't let you see anything . . . irregular.'

'So why can we see this?' said Jo.

'Perhaps you're special?' said Little Tragedy, winking at Jo.

'I don't think we're very special," said Will.

'We've never seen any of this until today,' said Jo.

She looked round. Will followed her gaze. The only thing more disconcerting than being attacked by dragons or calmly talking about it with moving statues was the fact they were doing this on a pavement surrounded by normal looking people who didn't move at all. He found it easier to focus on the statues and try not to see the people, somehow. Trying to make sense of them both together involved an unpleasant kind of twist in his head that made him very queasy.

'Well, today is a first,' said Victory. 'Because something has stopped time, and all the other Regulars with it.'

She too looked round at the normal people, still as a 3D snapshot all around them, the pedestrians, the children in the park, the drivers. The regular world. Frozen.

'Except us,' said Jo.

'So you must be special,' insisted Victory.

'Or irregular,' grinned Little Tragedy. 'What larks, eh?'

'We're not special,' said Will. 'Or irregular.'

'We're just frightened,' said Jo.

'And confused,' said Will. 'We don't know what to do.'

'Can you help us?' said Jo.

'I can't help,' said Victory. 'I know nothing more than you for now. But here will be a meeting of all the statues. When there's a crisis, there's always a meeting to see what can be done.'

'Where?' began Jo.

'Will you take us there,' said Will, cutting in.

Victory looked at Ariel and shook her head.

'I cannot,' she said. 'I must take Ariel home to

her plinth.'

'But we're in danger!' said Jo. 'An angel would help us.'

'I'm not an angel,' said Victory. 'And Ariel is in danger.'

'She's dead,' said Jo. 'Sorry. But we're not.'

'She's only dead today,' said Little Tragedy. Victory looked at the darkening sky with the beginnings of impatience.

'If any of us are hurt but put back on our plinths by midnight then we revive and all our wounds are healed,' she said. 'I must take her. You can help yourselves. Tragedy will guide you. And take that shield.'

She gave Little Tragedy a severe look.

'You know where to take them if they want angels.'

''Course I do,' he said, 'I'll take 'em to the Prudentials. Couple of useful Georges there too, and all. But . . .'

'No buts. They'll be safe enough there until the Tithing tonight,' said Victory. 'And no jokes, no fibs and no detours. I'm counting on you to be your good self.'

The look that passed between them was precisely the one a parent would give a habitually naughty child.

'He'll take good care of you,' said Victory walking

back to Will and Jo. 'No malice in him, but he is easily distracted, so watch him.'

She leant in and spoke very quietly, so that Tragedy couldn't hear.

'He's lonely. Always looking for playmates. The real tragedy of Little Tragedy is he wants a gang, but no one will play with him for long. He's very young under his cocky exterior. His bravado's about as thin as that mask he carries around. He gets upset if he thinks he's being left out or left on his own, but be nice to him and he's loyal as a puppy.'

Will thought she looked like she was hiding a smile, but then she looked back up into the sky as if smelling a change in the wind.

'The dragons will know that one is hurt. They will come for him too to get him to his plinth. You should go now. They will not forgive you for hurting one of their own. And there are more dangerous things than dragons abroad.'

Jo and Will looked in the direction she was staring.

A bird was circling in the air a long way off.

'It's a hawk,' said Will. 'Just a bird.'

'But no other birds are flying,' said Victory pointedly. 'The pigeons, the sparrows, all frozen in time too . . .'

And then she grasped the twisted torso of Ariel around the waist as her wings unfolded and flapped her into the sky.

'Wait!' said Will. 'Please!'

Victory kept rising into the air.

'Go now,' she said. 'I will likely see you at The Tithing.'

Jo and Will exchanged a look of controlled panic.

'What about Mum,' said Jo, looking across at where their mum was still running motionlessly in the frozen traffic.

'Can't leave her like that,' said Will. He looked over his shoulder.

The hawk was still circling a long way off, but there was something he didn't like about it.

'We can't move her,' he said. 'Jo. She'll be safe there for now.'

Then he picked up the wheelchair and put their mother back on her feet, on the pavement.

'That your mum?' said Little Tragedy.

Jo nodded.

'Luck-y!' said Little Tragedy. 'I never had a mum. What's it like then?

Jo swallowed.

'It's good,' said Will.

'It's nice,' said Jo.

'Bet it is,' said Tragedy wistfully. 'I didn't get a father neither . . .'

For a moment they all looked at Will and Jo's mother. Will wished more than anything that their dad was there too. Then the moment was broken by Little Tragedy snorting up a chuckle.

'Tell you what though, it ain't half a laugh seeing you lot all still as statues for a change, eh? Whole world's gone vicey-versa, and for all we know up'll be down before we know it. Come on slowcoaches,' he said. 'Keep up. It won't help your old mum if we get flamed by a dragon, will it? Let's do what Victory said.'

Jo looked at Will, and then she got in the wheelchair.

'We're going to be OK,' she said. 'Right, Will?'

'Right,' he said.

'Promise?'

He nodded.

'Promise.'

'Don't make promises you can't keep,' said Little Tragedy. 'You killed a dragon, and now you're nicking its shield. We're in big trouble if they catch us.'

Will shrugged and slung the shield over his back.

'You could leave it,' said Jo.

'Don't think that'd make up for killing the dragon,' said Will, pushing forward. 'And the truth is, the shield makes me feel stronger. Don't know why.'

He picked up speed. It was true. The shield did seem to give him more strength. He needed it to keep up with Tragedy who was jogging ahead of them and beckoning for them to follow as he ran.

'Stronger is good,' she said. 'Trust him?'

'Don't know,' said Will. 'He's just a kid really.'

'Loyal as a puppy doesn't sound very reassuring does it? Puppies are all over the shop till you train them,' she whispered. 'See the horns?'

'Oh yes,' he said bouncing off the curb and round a corner.

'Watch it!' she said.

'Hold on and you'll be fine,' he gritted, as his legs pistoned into a sprint. Tragedy was peering round the next corner as if to see if the coast was clear. He looked back, flashed a grin, and waved them on.

Will looked up into the sky and had the nasty feeling the hawk had just flown closer.

He wondered if he'd just lied to Jo for the second time in a minute.

He had no idea if they were going to be safe. And he was pretty sure the hawk was trouble.

7

The Eye of Horus

The stone hawk hung in the air, wings stretched wide, cutting slow circles across the sky as its unblinking eyes scanned the city streets.

From this high London did not look like a map. It did not look like anyone had planned it at all. It looked like an accident, a mess of roofs jumbled together without any rhyme and no more reason than the contents of a crammed toy-box would have shown if they'd been dumped out onto the floor by a fretful child.

The river writhed through the city in a series of powerful curves, like a thick brown snake, but apart from the choppy flow of the water, nothing was moving in the glimpsed streets beneath.

And that is what the hawk's eye was looking for.

Movement.

Hawks are not praised for their wisdom, like owls. They are not prized for their song, like nightingales.

They are feared for their purpose, which is to spy from on high, and then stoop to kill. Hawks are feared because they are hunters, and rightly so. They have no mercy, no gentleness, no remorse. Hawks are death-from-the-sky.

On the edge of its field of vision something flickered.

The hawk blinked the blue disk of its eye and tipped its wings, drifting silently across the evening air towards the spot where the stillness had been momentarily broken.

Deep in the Ancient Egyptian Gallery of the British Museum, a mile away, nothing was moving, except shadows. The four lion-women were now on their hands and knees looking down into the black stone coffin with intense concentration; the band round the outside was still glowing with blue light, and the hieroglyphics within seemed to be moving like agitated stick-cartoons.

The lion-women ignored them entirely, concentrating on the inside of the stone coffin which was carved out in a rough man-shape.

It had – like the bath it resembled – been filled with water. It was – unlike a bath – showing the four lion-women everything the hawk was seeing, like a screen projected on the inky surface of the liquid. The blueish light coming from it was sending the shadows dancing across the walls and ceiling.

The image disappeared for a fraction of a second as the hawk blinked.

'There,' said one of the lion-women. 'It has seen something.'

'THE HAWK IS THE SKY,' said the strange everywhere-voice that came from nowhere, or from all of them at once despite the fact that their mouths did not move. 'THE SKY CONTAINS THE SUN AND THE MOON, WHICH ARE ITS EYES. SUN AND MOON SEE EVERYTHING.'

The lion-women bent closer over the sarcophagus to examine the picture playing across the surface of the liquid within. They looked rather less like women and considerably more like lionesses gathered at a water-hole. The small cat, a bronze statue whose golden earrings and matching nose-rings marked it as a considerably tamer and very distant cousin of the four huntresses, purred beneath their bodies, twining in and out of their arms and legs. They paid it no mind.

They were concentrating on what the hawk's eye was showing them. The huntresses were sharing the hunter's eye and quivering with sympathetic anticipation as it swooped lower.

Again the hawk saw movement, and this time it was close enough for them to see that what it saw was a boy running along a street, pushing a girl in a wheelchair. They ran out of the hawk's view as they turned into a narrow lane, but they had been visible for long enough to recognize them

'People. Moving,' said the lion-woman with the stick. 'People should all be held unmoving by the Great Curse.'

Four pairs of cats' eyes lifted from the scene below them and met across the inky water.

'THE GREAT CURSE IS OUR POWER. THE GREAT CURSE IS OUR REVENGE. WE HAVE FROZEN TIME. ITS CHILDREN ARE ALL STILL. THESE TWO MUST BEAR SOME PROTECTION. THEY ARE NOT STILL. THIS IS NOT ACCEPTABLE.'

'What shall we do?' said the stick bearer.

'THE HAWK MUST GO TO THE DRAGONS. THE DRAGONS MUST NOT FAIL US A SECOND TIME.'

'Kill the children?'

'BRING THE CHILDREN. SEE WHAT THEIR PROTECTION IS. FOR IT CAN BE USED

AGAINST US. THEN DESTROY IT.'

'Then kill the children?'

There was a pause. The small cat, unconcerned by the debate going on above it and the unanswered question, looked down into the hawk's eye-view of London roof-tops gliding away beneath it, and then dipped a paw into the water. The ripples destroyed the mirror-like surface and the image disappeared.

The lion-women sighed and straightened up, going from four legs back to two.

The everywhere-voice answered the question with a quiet laugh that was too sinister to have much humour in it.

'KILL THE CHILDREN? HUNTERS MUST DO WHAT HUNTERS DO.'

8

Taken

As he ran through the streets pushing Jo in the wheelchair – which was getting heavier the further they ran after Little Tragedy – Will was learning something new about being terrified: when something frightening happens and keeps on happening, you do get more and more scared to start with. But as it goes on, the upward curve of your fear ceases to rise, and flattens, so you just stay at a constant level of fear. You can't keep getting even *more* scared indefinitely because you'd probably explode your head or something, so the fear levels off and stays the same, and then because it stays the same something really interesting happens. You get used to it.

He was beginning to be able to think straight.

They ran past a church front, old weathered grey stone with green moss stains running down from the turreted edge of the tower. A wedding party was just emerging. The bride and the groom looked radiantly happy as they walked out onto the steps into a frozen cloud of multi-coloured confetti and petals and rice that the guest were throwing.

The confetti cloud hung across the pavement blurring the view ahead like a soft but vivid mist. Tragedy just ran straight through it with a laugh. As they were right behind him they saw him cut a clean urchin-shaped tunnel through the static storm of bright scraps suspended in the air. He turned and beckoned them after him.

'Come on! S'only paper!'

They could see that, because all the confetti he had run through was now stuck to his front, making him look for an instant like a multi-hued *papier-maché* boy. Then Will pushed on through the confetti and they themselves emerged with a liberal coating of their own.

'Ugh,' spat Jo. 'Should have closed my mouth!'

Will wiped paper shreds off his face and kept going.

The flat fronts of the Georgian houses on this street were all sooty brick, and the white painted stone that surrounded the windows and doors was dingy with exhaust fumes. It had been a pretty street in its day, but a century of motor cars had turned it into one of the clogged, dirty arteries of London. The pavement was almost empty, and they were able to pick up speed as Will had no need to slalom round frozen pedestrians.

'Why's he going down here?' said Jo, craning back in the chair to look at Will as the wheels thrummed and jiggled across more uneven pavement. His face was red and sweating with the effort of running whilst pushing the wheelchair in front of him.

'HEY!' Will shouted, as Little Tragedy disappeared round a corner into a narrow lane. After a beat the impish face reappeared and waited for them.

'Why are we taking such a wiggly route,' he panted in irritation as he slowed to turn the corner into a street that was even narrower than the side street Tragedy'd just ducked them down.

'Safer,' said Tragedy. 'Your face is all red. You aren't cross are you?'

He looked unsettled by the thought, suddenly not so impish and much younger than normal.

'I'm doing my best,' he explained. 'It's safer, see . . .'

'Doesn't feel safer,' Jo said, looking up at the walls crowding in on them from both sides.

'I saw the hawk,' Tragedy said, setting off again. 'It might be, er, safer when we can't see the hawk.'

'It's just a bird,' she said.

'And a dragon's just a statue. Until it comes alive,'

puffed Will, grimacing as he tried to keep up with Tragedy. 'Nothing's normal today, and that includes the birds. Because there aren't any.'

'What's wrong with you,' she said, craning back to look at him. 'Why are you making that weird face.'

He was suddenly cross with her again, so cross that he actually felt as if he'd been cross with her for a very long time but hadn't quite noticed exactly how much, which made him doubly irritated. The feeling came at him all at once, like a giant wave. He felt almost as surprised as he felt angry. It was such a strong feeling that it left a sour taste in his mouth.

He came to a sudden halt. Jo had to grab the armrests to stop herself tumbling forward out of the chair.

'Watch out, you doofus!' she yelped, then saw his expression. 'What?'

'I'm making that weird face because I've got a stitch,' he said, breathing hard. 'And I've got a stitch because I'm pushing you all around London while you just sit there because you can't—'

He clamped his teeth on the ugly words before they could hop out of his mouth like a toad, but he needn't have bothered. Jo's face coloured right up, looking as red as his felt.

85

'Because I can't walk properly,' she said. 'Right?'

'Didn't say that,' he mumbled.

Tragedy ran back and looked at them both. He hopped from one foot to the other, as if he suddenly had to pee.

'Come on,' he said. 'All chums eh? Don't argue. Gets me nervy when people argue . . .'

Will looked up and met Jo's eyes.

'I didn't say that,' he said thickly.

'Yeah you did,' she said, levering herself out of the chair and catching her balance on the walking stick.

'You just didn't have the guts to say it out loud.'

She strode jerkily away from him. He followed her. 'No, no, come on, this isn't good,' cried Little Tragedy. 'We're mates, right, we're a gang, we shouldn't be arguing, arguing's what grown-ups do. We're not grown-ups are we? We're better than that!'

Will barely heard him. He only fleetingly noticed how upset the small boy was getting and then discarded the thought. Jo just marched lopsidedly off.

Will's own anger didn't just magically evaporate because he felt bad about what he'd nearly said. He still felt he was a coward who had lied. That just made it all curdle in his gut. In fact he felt angrier because he felt bad about being angry in the first place.

Nothing was fair.

'Jo,' he said. 'Look. Wait . . .'

She turned another corner without looking back.

He trotted after her into a sort of courtyard where someone had had the bright idea of squeezing a mini-park and recreation area into a space that was not nearly big enough for just one, let alone both of them.

Now it was Tragedy's turn to follow them, awkwardly pushing the discarded wheelchair ahead of him, even though he was too short to manage it properly.

'Hold up!' he panted. 'Here, I got your chair. Stick together, we got to stick together!'

Jo turned and leaned against a sign reading 'Old Gloucester Street Gardens (Alf Barrat Playground)'.

Gardens they might have once been in a long distant past, but right now there was not a blade of real grass in sight. The Gardens were divided in two, one half covered in a sickly green mat of faded astroturf on which were bolted outside versions of exercise machines you'd normally expect to see inside a gym, painted an even sicklier shade of lime than the plastic grass.

On the other side of a low fence was the children's playground, with a metal climbing frame that was a series of barred cages painted in funhouse primary colours. Beyond this was a swing-set on which a solitary child was frozen at the very end of her swing, her feet pointing to the sky and her back parallel with the ground. In front of her was a merry-go-round on which her parents, also unmoving, sat watching her with smiles stuck on their faces.

It was a dank, sad place, the opposite of Coram's Fields. In fact if Coram's Fields was one of the gloried 'Lungs of London' as the great parks were known, this was more like an abscess, one of those accidental voids created by the basic disorder of the city. It felt not just accidental but ignored, even by the blank-eyed windows and balconies that faced it.

'You know *why* my leg doesn't work?' she said, voice dangerously calm.

This was the conversation they never had.

Tragedy creaked up with the wheelchair, opened his mouth to say something, then shut it as he saw the deadly seriousness in their faces. Somehow this made him very agitated: his eyes widened and darted from one to the other.

'Course I do. Don't be stupid,' Will said. 'Come on, get in the chair.'

'I jumped onto that roof,' she said.

He didn't know why she was telling him this. Did she think *he* was stupid?

'I was there,' he said. 'Remember?'

'I know you were there,' she spat. 'You had to have been, because you dared me to jump didn't you?'

So here it was, Will thought. Here it comes. He felt curdled and tired and just not a bit interested in having this out right now, not now, not on top of everything else.

'I don't know what's going on,' said Little Tragedy, quavering a bit, 'Why are your voices going all funny?'

'You want me to say sorry?' Will said, ignoring him.

She hit him.

'No!' cried Tragedy, 'No hitting, no biting and no scratching! Them's the rules! Them's always the rules! You're upsetting me!'

Will staggered backwards feeling the side of his face where her fist had landed right beside his nose.

'Hey!' he said.

She looked almost as shocked by what she had done as he did.

'I jumped first,' he said, feeling the anger spike in his nostrils. 'I didn't make you do anything I hadn't done . . .'

She hit him again. He felt his fist bunch, even

though there were good rules about hitting girls. He opened it and jabbed an accusing finger at her instead.

'You're a nutter!' he shouted. 'You hit me again and I'll—'

He didn't know what he'd do. Even though sisters weren't exactly girls like other girls were, the same rules applied. He turned to look at Little Tragedy. He wasn't there. All there was was the wheelchair.

'Where'd he go,' he said, an ominous pit opening up in his stomach. 'Jo—'

'Who cares?' she said, her blood still up, eyes blazing. 'It's not about him.'

'I know,' he said, eyes flicking up to the sky.

'It's about you!' she said, her voice thick. 'Do you know why I wanted you to say sorry?'

'No,' he said, turning in a full circle, searching for Tragedy, who had completely disappeared. He had a bad feeling about this. 'No I don't.'

'You're so ANNOYING!' she shouted.

'FINE.' he shouted back. 'I'm sorry. I'm sorry I made you jump!'

'YOU DIDN'T MAKE ME JUMP!' she yelled, right into his face, with such force he felt the fine spray of her spit on his cheek. 'That's what's so

ANNOYING: you're such a bighead that you think it's all about you! You think you can make me do things just by saying stuff, like I'm a silly little girl!'

He could see the strings on her neck, whip-tight and quivering with tension.

'You. Didn't. Make. Me. Jump,' she said, prodding him in the chest to emphasise each word. 'You just dared me! It was my choice. I could have said no! I *chose* to do the stupid thing. Not you. Because you know what Will? You're not the boss of me.'

He said nothing. This irritated her even more. She rolled her eyes and stepped back.

'You're so up yourself. Sometimes I really hate you.'

'Yeah?' he said, feeling his nose.

'Yeah,' she said, 'you can be a real pain. You're not even a whole year older than I am and yet you always act like you're in charge.'

They stared at each other.

'Yeah?'

Her mouth was a tight slash.

'Yeah,' she said.

He nodded.

'Yeah. Well, I hate you too.'

Even as he said it he felt littler. He felt meaner, less himself, more like a baby, worse than the coward he knew himself to be. Even as he said it he wished he hadn't, so he tried to take the edge off it by adding:

'. . . sometimes.'

But sometimes is too late. Sometimes you can't take things back. This needed more. And he knew what that was: he had to tell her. It was time. It might make things worse, probably would. But at least it wouldn't fester. At least he could just get on with being a coward without adding to the rotten feeling by also being a liar. He grabbed her arm and held on.

'Look. If it makes you feel better, I hate myself all the time . . .'

'It doesn't,' she spat bitterly. 'Just shows you're a good judge of character.'

She tried to wrench her arm free. He realized she wasn't going to make this easy. But he was going to do it. Everything would start getting better if he did it. He was as sure as anything he'd ever been sure about in his life.

'Fine. But I hate myself because I was a coward. And a liar.' He began to feel cleaner even as he got the hard words out of himself. 'What you don't know about the accident is—'

Sometimes even confessions are too late. This was one of those times, because in between telling her she didn't know something and going on to tell her what that was, there was a gap as he steeled himself to tell the final truth that would make or break their relationship forever and into that gap the first dragon dropped off the roof . . . and attacked her.

Will never knew if she had time to hear him try and take the edge off what he'd said because the second dragon launched off the roof behind him in a great clatter of metal wings that gave him just enough time to turn and get the shield up before being knocked flat beneath it.

He didn't see the first dragon close a talon around Jo's waist and yank her upwards.

He did hear her yell in shock.

He didn't see her try and grab the iron railing. He didn't see her try and club the dragon with her stick, though he did hear the smack it made against the side of its head.

He didn't see any of that because he was squashed beneath the shield with another angry dragon on top of it, trying to wrench it loose and get at him. He was holding on so tight that he didn't see his sister's hand ripped free of the railing as the first dragon's greater strength took over, nor did he see her friendship bracelet scrape against the iron top of the rail and rip free.

And because he was so busy fighting for his own life he did not see her stiffen and freeze, so that the dragon scrabbled up onto the second floor balcony overlooking the gardens with something in its talon that was suddenly more like a stiff doll than the living person it had surprised moments before.

Her mouth was open in mid yell, and her eyes were wide, but she was as frozen as everyone else in the city.

Everyone else except for her brother.

Will saw the talons of his own dragon curl around the shield and felt his muscles ache as he tried to resist their unyielding strength. He felt like an oyster must feel as someone levers the lid off their shell. He knew exactly how soft and exposed he was going to be the moment he let go.

He did see Jo's stick clatter to the ground next to him.

The sight of it filled him with dread, and the fear spiked his adrenaline. Without knowing why he did it, or even how he did it, he did the only thing that enabled him to remain free for the next few seconds.

He didn't let go of the shield. He used every ounce

of strength in his arms to push it in the direction the dragon was pulling, and then let go.

The dragon tumbled back in surprise as it yanked the shield into its own nose with such force that it lay on its back and shook its head in stunned shock. Then it roared and leapt for the spot on the sickly green outdoor carpet where Will had been.

Only Will was no longer there. He had rolled and bounced to his feet, hurdling the low railings into the playground and diving for the protective bars of the metal climbing frame.

He rolled in under the platform as the Dragon hurled the useless shield at him. It hit the bars with enough force to bend them and shower Will with paint flakes, but he was safe.

'Jo!' he shouted, scuttling this way and that, his neck craned as he looked up, trying to catch a glimpse of his sister before the dragon renewed its attack.

He saw her clutched in the other dragon's talon, rigid and unmoving as his captor snarled a dismissive roar at him.

'Jo!' he shouted in despair.

9

Delivered by Dragon

The dragon carrying Jo landed in front of the great façade of the museum, swayed up the shallow steps between the pillars and banged on the open door with a bunched talon, peering into the gloom within.

As it waited, it gave Jo an irritable little shake, but she did not move a muscle. She was as stiff as a board. Whatever had protected her from being frozen like everyone else in the city was now clearly not working.

'DON'T BREAK IT,' said the everywhere-voice. The dragon looked up. The inner hall was still full of nothing but frozen people and shadows. 'WE WANT TO SEE WHY IT WAS WALKING WHEN ALL THE OTHER CHILDREN OF TIME ARE AT REST.'

Then some of the shadows moved and became the stone lion-women. One of them walked up to the dragon and took Jo from its grip, turning her this way and that, almost as if she was looking for a switch. Then it held her close to its nostrils and smelled her.

'She is nothing special,' she said, turning to look at the others.

The cat appeared, looking bored as usual as it twisted between the legs of the lion-women. It lifted a paw and casually batted Jo's shoe, which was hanging a foot off the ground as the statue held her in the air. Then it walked away, uninterested.

'THEN IT IS THE BOY,' said the everywhere-voice. All the lioness heads turned and looked at each other. 'TAKE THE GIRL. PUT HER IN THE SARCOPHAGUS SO WE MAY QUESTION HER. IT MAY BE WE NEED TO USE HER TO BREAK HIM.'

As the one holding Jo walked away towards the Great Court one of the other lion-women walked up to the dragon and put a hand on its shoulders and looked deep into its eyes. The blue light blazing out of her own eyes sharpened and focused into a beam.

'All the City dragons can hear me through you,' it said.

It wasn't a question.

'All dragons. Find the boy. Bring him to us now. Do not fail us.'

The dragon made as if to leave.

The lioness held it steady.

For a moment the dragon looked surprised. And then, as the blue light beaming into its eyes intensified, it began to shake. The light seemed to liquefy and spill out of its eye sockets, running in thick streams down its silver scales, spiralling around its torso and dripping down its arms and legs.

The dragon's spikey ears went flat like a dog being punished, and it began to whine in pain.

It was not used to being frightened, or hurt. And from the way the whines mounted shrilly and then abruptly changed to low whimpers, it was clear that the lion-woman was causing it a great deal of pain.

The dragon dropped first to one knee, then the other, and then reached out a stubby claw to try and stop itself falling sideways into the pillar. It slumped against it and held on, talons scrabbling at the smooth stone curve, trying to keep a grip.

The lioness let go and stepped back.

Instantly the blue liquid covering the dragon disappeared as the connection was broken and it slid off the pillar and fell back down the steps in an untidy jumble of wings and whimpering.

'Do not fail us again. Or you will all feel the Pain of

Sekhmet,' said the lioness, turning to rejoin the shadows within.

'Bring the boy before midnight.'

10

The Fusilier

Tragedy had led them into a trap. Probably not on purpose, but accidentally he had bottled them up in a space almost entirely constructed from dead-ends.

Will couldn't really blame the little imp for running off and saving himself. He too wished he was away, instead of stuck here.

Hiding in the cage under the climbing frame was not the most sensible thing to have done. Will could see that now. When he ran – a moment ago that already felt like a lifetime – he hadn't planned further ahead than getting to a place of immediate safety.

On the plus side the bars around him were sturdy. They had already stopped the hurtling metal shield the dragon had spun at him. Without the bars to save him, Will would probably have lost his head already.

But the problem with the bars, brightly painted though they were, was that they were bars: bars have, by definition, gaps between them. Bars can stop big solid things, but they're not so good with other stuff.

Like fire.

Dragons, on the other hand, are very good with fire.

Will could see the dragon was building heat inside the crop in its neck. The silver painted metal was beginning to blush pink with the growing pressure of the wildfire trapped beneath it. Curly tendrils of smoke were starting to emerge from its nostrils.

Will reached through the bars, trying to scrabble a hand-hold on the shield, hoping against hope that he would be able to repeat the trick he'd used last time, redirecting the jet of flame back on the dragon, but as he got his fingers on the very lip of it the dragon stepped forward and jabbed a single talon down onto the other side of the shield and very deliberately scraped it back just out of his reach. It did so with a kind of controlled malice in its eye, its lip curled into a sneer.

He scrabbled backwards. The other thing about a cage is that though it's only averagely good for certain kinds of protection, it's *very* good for being trapped in. If the dragon started blasting fire he was going to be burned to a crisp.

He scooted through a narrow gap and stood poised

to dodge either way, keeping the climbing frame between him and the dragon.

The dragon stepped sideways and just stared at him.

It looked amused.

Will edged further to his left, so that the broad steel slide that came off the upper level of the climbing frame was blocking the dragon's view of everything but his head.

He was going to have to run.

It was hopeless anyway, but his dad once told him that a moving target was harder to hit, and whether or not that was true, there was no question that if he stood still he was toast.

At least on the outside. Outside he'd be burned and crispy. Inside he'd probably still be squishy. But cooked. Like a marshmallow at a bonfire party.

Yes.

He'd have to move. If he could get six metres to his left, running past the swing-set with its weirdly frozen girl sticking out into mid-air, there was a wall. He thought he could jump and scramble himself over, and then he could perhaps find shelter in the narrow space between it and the houses behind.

There was a clang and a scrape as the dragon put its front foot on the slide, testing it. It was in no hurry. It knew it had him.

It slid back a bit, but stopped itself by jagging the talons of its foot into the thin sheet of metal, punching holes as easily as if it were paper.

That wasn't good either.

In two steps it was on top of the climbing frame, looking straight down at him.

All that Will could think of doing to distract it was bound to fail. It was bound to fail because it was the oldest trick in the book.

But sometimes the oldest trick is the only one left.

Sometimes it's all you have.

Will looked to the left of the dragon and waved frantically.

'Hey, yes! Help me!!'

The dragon turned to see who was there, and Will ran.

He ran faster than he'd ever run before, 0–60 in two strides, muscles bouncing and legs pumping like trip hammers as he punched forward through the air, heading for the brick wall beyond the swings.

He heard the dragon roar behind him, but that didn't make him look round. It made him run faster. It made him jump higher. It made his outstretched hands hold the top of the wall in a stronger grip, and it made his arms pull his body over the top in one fluid movement.

What it didn't do was make him drop to safety on the other side of the wall.

There was no drop.

And that's where his plan hit its own particular wall and stopped dead.

There was a flat roof, a dank mossy expanse of roofing felt with a shallow puddle in the middle of it. He slid to an embarrassing halt in the scrape of water, wet and painfully aware that the only thing between him and a very angry dragon was the lip of the wall, maybe 15 centimetres tall, enough to have hidden the treacherous roof behind, but no use for hiding anything else.

He scrabbled back until he hit the façade of the house and stared at the lip of the wall.

He couldn't see the dragon.

Then he saw twin tendrils of smoke rise up over the edge of the bricks. And then he saw the silver-painted ears, and then the angry red little eyes pop up and stare at him, and then the wings cracked out behind it and the dragon's neck and chest came into view, and now that he had tried the oldest trick in the book his list of options seemed to be terminally blank.

He'd run himself into a corner with no way out. The wall behind him was solid. It felt like the end.

He caught a glimpse of the shield he had dropped on the green astroturf behind the dragon. He should not have dropped it. Just another in a long line of stupid mistakes that had got him here. He was drowning in a sea of mistakes.

'Stupid,' he said. 'Really stupid.'

The dragon cocked its head. Suddenly he had a thought. And when you're drowning every thought is like a life-belt. So he grabbed at it and clung on, and the thought was this: he wondered how stupid the dragon really was. It was deadly, sure, but might it not also be a bit . . . thick? After all. it had fallen for the oldest trick in the book once. Maybe it would—

He pointed over its wings.

'Look!' he said. 'Behind you!!'

The dragon was not that stupid.

It shook its head, drew it back like a snake about to strike and then jerked it forward, mouth starting to open screamingly wide – so wide he saw the fireball beginning to roil out of its gullet and jet towards him—

BLAM

The gunshot echoed round the narrow courtyard,

and the dragon's head was knocked sideways by the impact of the bullet, so that the wildfire jerked and hit the wall just to Will's right. His arm was splashed by the fire, but the bullet saved him, stopping it from taking the full blast. As the flames bit into his coat and the arm beneath, he dropped and rolled into the puddle, which extinguished the fire in a damp sizzle. As he did this the jet of flame made a long fiery paint splash for the next five metres as the dragon's head continued to move, until—

BLAM

The second bullet hit it in the body, knocking its legs out from under it so that the head suddenly disappeared as it dropped like a stone, hitting its chin on the lip of the wall, snapping its neck upwards with a sharp crack as it disappeared from view. The last that Will saw of it was a final burst of wildfire vomitted straight into the air like a blazing fountain that geysered upwards before making a nearly perfect umbrella shape, and falling straight back down to earth.

Will didn't move.

He'd seen it. His ears had heard the gunshots. His brain had just not managed to take it in.

'You still with us then, nipper?' said a man's voice with a cockney edge to it.

Will scrambled to the edge of the wall and looked down.

A statue was looking up at him. It was a soldier in a First World War uniform, made of brass that was black with age and spattered with pigeon mess much as Victory had been. He had a tin helmet and a pack, and was standing over the sprawled and immobile dragon with his rifle pointing at its head. There was a long and very pointy bayonet, almost like a sword, fixed on the end of the gun.

He had one eye on the dragon and one on Will.

'There you are. Good. Thought this blighter might have roasted yer . . .'

The dragon tried to lift its head.

Without thinking the soldier lunged and stabbed the dragon.

'No no,' he gritted. 'Can't be having that, matey. 'Cos my mother said . . .'

Stab.

'. . . you shouldn't go aroun' . . .'

Stab.

'. . . trying to roast up little boys . . .'

Stab.

'. . . all aroun' the town.'

And with that he put a hobnailed boot on the

dragon's neck and yanked the long sword-bayonet free for the last time.

Wildfire spilled out of the wound, its energy spent, dribbling like a liquid, pooling on the ground around the dragon's head, melting the sickly green astroturf before dying out entirely.

The soldier looked at his bayonet, then down at the dragon.

'Ugly brute, isn't he?'

Will's mouth worked silently.

'Something you want to say?'

Will swallowed.

'Who are you?' he said.

The soldier tipped back his helmet and fixed his eyes on Will's with a stern look.

'That's the first thing you want to say is it?'

He scratched his chin. He looked very grim.

'Oh well. Kids these days, eh? Ain't got the manners of a butcher's dog, have you?'

Will swallowed. The soldier exhaled and shrugged

'Who am I? Well sonny, I'm Corporal thank-you-very-much-for-saving-my-bacon-from-the-big-nasty-dragon-that-was-trying-to-turn-my-ungrateful-little-hide-into-nice-crispy-pork-crackling is who I am.'

Will felt his cheeks burn with embarrassment. The

soldier relaxed his face a millimetre, so that it at least looked like a face that *could* smile, maybe one day in the long distant future, even though it wasn't letting much of that show right now.

A familiar voice piped up from behind the big soldier.

'But you can call him Fusilier. Everyone else does.'

Will's jaw dropped in surprise. It was Little Tragedy, grinning so wide his face was close to splitting.

'Right,' said Will. 'I mean thank you. For saving my bacon. Hide. You know . . .'

'I do know,' agreed The Fusilier, hanging his gun over his shoulder by the sling. 'Same as I know you should thank this little devil for coming and getting me.'

Will looked at Tragedy who was beaming back at him, hopping nervously from foot to foot.

'Thank you Tradge,' said Will.

'Pleasure,' he replied, and then he put the sad mask over his face, 'And I'm sorry about your sister an' all.'

Will nodded. All the relief at having survived the dragon drained out of his boots at the mention of Jo, and he felt suddenly very shaky and hollow. The Fusilier looked at him closely.

'Right chum. Need to get that arm seen to. We

'know just who to take you to, right Tradge?'

'You do?' asked Will. His arm was throbbing badly.

'Ho yes,' grinned Tragedy. 'What you need is a ministering bleedin' angel.'

'So come down off of that roof, careful like, keep your eyes peeled and follow me,' said The Fusilier.

'And don't argue,' said Little Tragedy. 'No more arguing please.'

Will rolled to the edge and lowered himself to the ground. It was very odd stepping over the dead dragon and seeing the happy smiling faces of the couple watching their daughter frozen on the swing, unaware of the mayhem that had just passed in front of their unseeing eyes.

'Right,' said The Fusilier. 'Let's scarper.'

Will remembered how he'd wished he'd kept hold of the shield, so he ran over and picked it up.

'Seriously sonny. We need not to be here,' said The Fusilier. 'Dragons are all brothers, least them silver ones are. They'll know something's up with one of theirs and be flocking over here for a look-see.'

'Come on,' said Tragedy. 'Why aren't you moving?'

'Wait,' said Will. His eyes had seen something else on the ground. 'Just wait a moment. Please.'

That wasn't the question, thought Will,

remembering how frozen and lifeless Jo had suddenly looked in the dragon's talons. He could move if he wanted to; it was Jo that wasn't moving. Why?

He knelt and pulled something familiar out from under one of the exercise bicycles.

It was Jo's bracelet.

He stared at it. Something clicked in his head, like a puzzle piece landing in place. He looked at the scarab on his wrist.

'What?' said Little Tragedy.

'I think I might know why Jo stopped moving,' said Will slowly.

'Who?' said The Fusilier.

'My sister. And I think that means I know why I'm moving and everyone else is frozen in time.'

11

Under the Blue Light

Jo's eyes blinked and she woke up. She was lying on the bottom of something with steep black sides. A couple of feet above her was a ceiling, not quite solid, like a layer of smoke with light rippling slowly across it, through which she could make out shapes bending over and looking down at her.

She had the terrifying thought that she was under water, but realized that couldn't be because she didn't feel wet and could breathe.

She did not feel strong enough to move much more than her hand, however, which reached up and touched the blue plane of light, making ripples as her fingers poked through it.

'Where am I?' she said.

The voice that answered her seemed to come from everywhere and nowhere at the same time, like a voice that bypassed her ears and spoke right inside her head.

'WHERE DO YOU THINK YOU ARE.'

'Hospital' she answered, without thinking.

She saw a hand reach down through the light and feel the brace on her knee. She was pleased that it was not aching. Maybe they'd given her something for the pain. Whoever they were. Wherever this was . . .

YOU HAVE BEEN HURT.

'Yes.'

'TELL US WHAT WE ASK AND WE WILL HURT THOSE WHO HURT YOU.'

Jo's heart bumped out of rhythm. Something was wrong with a voice that said things like that.

'This isn't a hospital.' She said.

'IT IS A PLACE OF SAFETY.'

'No it's not.'

'IT CAN'T BE.'

'Where's Will?'

She could feel fear welling up inside her.

'WHO IS WILL?'

'My—'

Jo tried to crush the fear by stopping talking and trying to think. She didn't want to give this voice anything. Not until she knew what was happening.

'AH.'

'Who are you?' she said.

'WILL IS THE BOY.'

113

'Who are you?'

'DID WILL HURT YOU?'

'No.'

The voice was like a purr. Gentle. Comforting, even.

'HE BETRAYED YOU.'

Dangerously soft. Like a cat with claws hidden but ready . . .

'No.'

'IF HE DID NOT BETRAY YOU, HOW DID YOU COME HERE?'

'You said this was a place of safety.'

The voice said nothing.

'So how can he have betrayed me by bringing me here, if this is somewhere safe?'

'SHARP GIRL. DON'T CUT YOURSELF ON YOUR CLEVERNESS.'

There they were. The claws.

'Who are you?' she asked carefully.

12

The Dark City

The sun had set. Will hadn't noticed exactly when, but as The Fusilier led them at a fast trot away from the gardens he realized the city had got much darker.

On reflex he pulled his phone and checked the time. It was stuck. The clock had not moved on from the moment he'd first seen the dragon back in the hospital window.

'What you doing, slowcoach?' said Tragedy. 'Keep up.'

'Checking the time,' he said.

'Only one thing you need to know about that,' said The Fusilier as he jinked round a corner in a controlled slide, the hobnails on his boots skating noisily sideways on the pavement. 'If the dragons are attacking you, it's already too late.'

'So what's this big secret you know?' said Little Tragedy. 'Why aren't you froze like the other Regulars?'

The Fusilier looked back over his shoulder and

raised an eyebrow.

Will felt Jo's bracelet in his pocket. He pulled it out and showed it to them. Then he shot his wrist out of his cuffs and showed his own bracelet.

'Bracelet?' said The Fusilier. 'I think it's more than jewellery, mate.'

'No,' said Will. 'It makes sense . . . When we were both wearing them, we weren't frozen. Then Jo's got torn off and she did freeze.'

He looked at them both. They didn't look convinced.

'It makes sense,' he repeated, hearing how weak that sounded second time round. Maybe he was just wanting it to be so because he needed *something* to make sense in the midst of all this scary craziness he was trapped in.

'OK then,' said The Fusilier. 'Take your bracelet off. See if you freeze.'

Will shook his head.

'I'll put it back on you,' smiled Little Tragedy encouragingly. 'Go on, give it a go!'

Maybe it was because his hair was pushed back revealing his little horns that made Will shake his head. He didn't seem quite trustworthy. Something that the Victory had said that stuck in his head:

Tragedy often meant well but wasn't quite reliable.

'What you scared of?' said The Fusilier.

'That it might *not* work.' said Will.

The Fusilier exhaled in frustration and shook his head.

'So why do you want to find your sister and put hers back on?'

'Because it *might* work,' said Will. 'Sorry. It makes sense to me.'

And it did. If there was a tiny chance he'd go to sleep on his feet like all these people in the street around him, the frozen taxi drivers and people on buses and bicycles and the crowd on the pavements they were moving through, he couldn't afford to take it. But if there was a tiny chance he could get Jo back and awake, he had to take it.

He slipped her bracelet back in his pocket and zipped it up. The Fusilier shrugged and led on. Tragedy tutted and shook his head at Will.

'You don't trust me,' he said. 'We're meant to be mates. I brought him back to save you!'

'Sorry,' said Will. He wasn't going to be guilted into doing it. Maybe he was too scared to try taking off his scarab bracelet in case it *didn't* work. Maybe he just needed the possibility he was right: maybe he was clinging to that straw because otherwise he would have nothing, and drown.

As they carried on he realized what was so extra creepy now that evening was on them: normally street lamps come on when it gets dark. Normally cars turn on their headlights and people in buildings turn on the lamps when the sun goes down. Normally it's so automatic that you don't even notice it. None of that had happened.

The buildings were taller now as they got closer to the centre of the City, big purpose-built office blocks replacing the two- or three-storey houses they had been passing. There were *some* lights on – traffic lights, some windows and a few cars that had the kind of lights that were on all the time, but that meant there was just enough light to throw deep shadows that made the darkness seem all the weirder and more threatening, and the road felt less like a street than a deep dark canyon.

The falling darkness sucked colour out of the world, and without colour the unmoving pedestrians looked all the more like statues and less like real people. And now they stopped looking like actual people who might spring back into action at any moment, it was like they were even more absent. Because of that

Will suddenly felt very alone indeed.

He looked sideways into the murky interior of a supermarket as he passed. People were black silhouettes standing at the till waiting to pay, backlit by the dim light of big fridges full of soft drinks and frozen produce. He had the nasty thought that maybe they'd be there forever, money in hands, queuing for eternity.

It also made him realize how dry his mouth was.

Then he had the slightly better thought that he could just go into a shop and take a can, and that thought led to the next, which was that, in other circumstances – circumstances that didn't include dragons or his sister and mother getting frozen in time – this should be fun. He could go into any shop and take anything. The city could, in those other circumstances, be the best game ever. Instead of the worst nightmare—

He ran straight into the back of The Fusilier. Which was painful. Partly because The Fusilier was made of bronze, mainly because he hit him with the arm that had been burned by the wildfire.

'Ouch,' he said, stumbling backwards, clutching it.

'Shhh,' said Tragedy as the Fusilier dropped to one knee behind a rubbish bin and motioned for Will and

Tragedy to get behind him.

He quickly unslung the rifle from his shoulder and aimed it over the top of the bin. Will watched him very quietly work the lever on the gun to put a bullet in the chamber, ready for firing. Tragedy flinched his eyes shut and stuck his fingers in his ears.

If Will's mouth had felt a little bit dry before, it now felt parched as a desert. He breathed shallowly and squinted in the direction the gun was pointed at. At first he couldn't see anything in the darkness and occasional slashes of light ahead, but then it shifted.

It was a shadow, and it was being thrown by something moving towards them from a side street on their left. It prowled forward silently with the ease of a predator, a big four-legged hunter, unmistakably feline and deadly.

'What is it?' whispered Will, very aware that something at the base of his brain was trying to tell his legs to get the rest of him as far from this corner as it could, as fast as possible.

'Tiger, I reckon,' said Tragedy. 'Looks like a tiger anyway.'

The Fusilier nodded.

'There's a big statue of a tiger out West, Victoria way. Must be that one. Can't think of any others.

Nasty blighter it is when it's riled.'

The shadow stopped and tensed, the long tail slowly curling over its back as it dropped its chest to the ground, back legs ready to spring.

'Heard us,' said The Fusilier. 'That's not good.'

He looked behind him and pointed to the open door of the shop with the queue in it.

'Back up slow,' he whispered.

'Can't you just shoot it?' breathed Will.

'I can shoot *at* it. And I can miss it, like as hit it,' hissed The Fusilier, easing back from the bin and waving him to do the same. 'Tiger moves faster than you can think and it'll need more than one round to put it down even if I get lucky. Step quiet now . . .'

They inched backwards, pace by silent pace.

They were halfway between the safety of the bin and the open door when the tiger moved – its shadow getting bigger and bigger as it neared the corner. Will forgot to breathe. His legs forgot not to start shaking.

The Fusilier risked a quick look behind to see how close they were and then snapped his head back to aim at the corner.

'Run,' he said. 'I'll nail it.'

Will's legs didn't need telling twice, but he and Tragedy were in such a hurry to be elsewhere that they

121

somehow got in each other's way as he turned to run, and they both stumbled and fell instead.

Pain jagged up his arm as he slapped the pavement with his hand, trying to stop himself, and then he was spread-eagled on the ground with no protection as the tiger leapt round the corner.

BLAM

The Fusilier's shot went high and missed.

Partly this was because he jerked the muzzle towards the sky at the last minute.

Partly it was because the big tiger wasn't either big, nor in fact a tiger.

It was a small house cat.

Not a real cat, true: a statue of a cat, but life-sized.

It stood there blinking at them in surprise.

'Hodge!' said The Fusilier. 'I nearly punched your ticket, you mug!'

'You know it?' said Will.

'Course I know it. Everyone knows it,' giggled Tragedy in relief. 'Most famous cat in London is that. It's Dictionary's cat.'

He uncocked his rifle and slung it over his shoulder as he walked towards the waiting cat.

'Here kitty—'

'Dictionary?' said Will. 'Who's he?'

'Dictionary Johnson,' said the Fusilier. 'Splendid old buffer, lives on a plinth down Aldwych way, but his cat's normally on a different plinth down Fleet—'

Little Tragedy grinned and bent down to pet the cat.

The cat leapt at his face and slashed its claws across it so powerfully that Tragedy dropped the mask he carried and shrieked in pain.

The shock of the sudden and unprovoked attack triggered a stream of angry and disbelieving profanities that The Fusilier hurled after the cat as it streaked across the road and was lost in the shadows beyond.

The Fusilier felt Little Tragedy's cheek and the three gouges that were now scratched across it. Tragedy was trying not to sob, but was clearly in shock.

'What the blinking blink was that for?' he said. 'Me and that cat's old friends. It's a right old softie normally. It's gone mad.'

'I should say,' said The Fusilier, looking over his head at Will as he retrieved his helmet. 'Homicidal maniac. Should have shot the ruddy thing.'

Tragedy sniffed and felt his wounded cheek.

'I don't like this.' He sniffed. 'I don't like any of this.'

The Fusilier nodded.

'Yep. World's gone to the dogs when even the cats go mad,' he said.

13

Above the Blue Light

The feline voice repeated the question.

Jo did not know the answer. She almost did, but her brain was not working properly. The voice was dangerously mesmerizing and insistent, as if it was also using tones and frequencies too deep for normal ears, but strong enough to make her heart begin to bump out of rhythm.

'WHY COULD YOU MOVE?'

'What?'

'WHY COULD YOU MOVE WHEN OTHERS IN THE CITY COULDN'T?'

It all came back to her.

Not in bits and bobs, but all at once, like a great slump of wet snow falling of a steep roof high above her. The weight of memory hit her and buried her, smothering her and cutting her off from everything, and for a long time she just fought wildly against it, thrashing in panic, trying to flail her mind free of the images that were trapping her and making it harder and harder to breathe, let alone think.

It was remembering to breathe that calmed her down.

She remembered the pain, the earlier pain from the operations on her knee, and she remembered her mum telling her how to calm her breathing and that everything else would follow, that the pain wouldn't go, not all at once, but if she thought that every time she exhaled a little bit of it would disappear then that would be how to control it and not let it be the boss.

Jo decided not to let the panic be the boss either, and breathed it out, breath by breath. It took concentration, but it worked.

She felt the voice waiting for her to surface.

'AH.'

'This isn't a safe place.'

'TELL ME YOUR NAME, AND I WILL TELL YOU MINE.'

Jo paused for a moment.

'Joanna.'

Only people she didn't know, or people she didn't much like called her Joanna. She wasn't going to give this voice her real name.

'JOANNA. AND WHO IS THIS JOANNA?

WHY ARE YOU SPECIAL?'

'I'm just a girl,' she said. 'Who are you?'

Two hands reached down through the surface and sat her up. Only when her head broke clear and emerged into the air did she realize with horror that she had been lying under water. It cascaded off her face and hair as she fishmouthed and stared about her. The four lion-women knelt on the edge of what she now realized was some kind of stone mummy's coffin. Their faces were cold and intense and focused on hers. A small cat with earrings stood on the back of a frozen museum worker who was bent in front of the sarcophagus.

This was the moment when Jo could have let the panic take her and sweep her off in its dark undertow.

She concentrated on breathing. She saw the blue light rippling shadows across the roof, and she caught glimpses of other statues and unmoving people all round her. It was somewhere she'd been before.

'NOW YOU KNOW US!'

The voice was an exulting growl.

Jo shook her head.

'No. I mean you're frightening, and you're statues and you're moving and everything. And I think this is the museum. But . . . I don't know you.'

The lion-women growled and looked at each other. The cat came forward and put its paws on the edge of the stone, looking up at them. As one, they all turned their faces to Jo's and leant in. She pushed back against the stone tub until she couldn't get any further from them.

The voice dripped with disgust.

'WHEN WE WERE BETRAYED WE WERE RULERS OF THE WORLD. WE WERE TRICKED INTO STONE AND PENNED THERE FOR THOUSANDS OF YEARS. AND NOW WE ARE FORGOTTEN SHARDS IN SOME BARBARIANS' TREASURE HOUSE.'

She felt the deep growl of rage as much as heard it.

'I AM BAST, WE ARE SEKHMET. LOOK UPON ME IN ALL MY SHAPES AND TREMBLE!'

'What do you want?' she said, after a long enough pause had made it clear that something was expected from her, and she had had enough time to batten down that rising panic again.

'WHAT WE HAD. WHAT WAS TAKEN FROM US. THE HOT SUN ON OUR BACKS AS WE HUNT. THE FEAR. THE GRATITUDE OF THOSE WE FEED AND THOSE WE SUFFER TO LIVE ANOTHER DAY. THE WORSHIP. WE

WOULD BE GODS AGAIN!'

Jo swallowed. She spoke hesitantly.

'Er. That's not really gong to happen. The world just isn't like that any more . . .'

'THE WORLD IS AS WE CHOOSE TO MAKE IT! WE HAVE WOKEN AND OUR ANCIENT MAGIC IS WAKENING TOO. LOOK AROUND YOU. YOU SIT IN THE VERY SOURCE. FEEL THE POWER. IT GROWS WITH EVERY HOUR.'

'But you can't just stop people moving. You can't just—'

One of the lion-women lunged forward, muzzle to nose with her, eyes wide in anger. Her mouth didn't move but the words echoed in Jo's skull.

'WE HAVE FROZEN PEOPLE JUST AS PEOPLE TRAPPED US INTO THE STONE THAT HELD US FOR SO LONG, SEEING BUT UNMOVING! TIME HAS BEEN OUR JAILER, AND NOW WE CONTROL TIME. DO NOT THINK TO TELL US WHAT IS POSSIBLE!'

'You can't just . . . stop people. It's like killing, I mean it *is* killing.'

'WHAT OF IT? DO YOU THINK WE ARE STRANGERS TO THE DEATH OF MULTITUDES? DO YOU EVEN KNOW WHY

THEY WORSHIPPED US? NO. YOU HAVE FORGOTTEN, YOU COLD BARBARIANS OF THE NORTH, BANISHED SO FAR FROM THE REAL WORLD OF SUN AND LIGHT THAT YOU THINK THE PALTRY LION IS KING OF ALL ANIMALS.'

'You—'

'DO NOT SPEAK WHEN BAST SPEAKS.'

The voice made her ears ring.

'A LION MAY BE KING. BUT A KING IS A WEAKLING NEXT TO A QUEEN, FOR THE LIONESS IS DEADLIER BY FAR, FOR IT IS SHE WHO DOES THE HUNTING. IT IS THE LIONESS WHO GIVES LIFE AND IT IS SHE WHO BRINGS DEATH, AND THAT IS WHY BAST THE LIONESS IS OLD QUEEN OF ALL THE YOUNGER POWERS, BAST AND HER LATER FACE, MIGHTY SEKHMET, AND THAT IS WHY WE WILL RULE AGAIN! DO YOU UNDERSTAND?'

'Yes . . .'

'GOOD. THEN BOW.'

'. . . you're mad.'

'BE SILENT. BOW!'

And the strangest thing, amidst all this uncanny

weirdness, was that even if she had wanted to, which she didn't, Jo found she couldn't. She thought of pretending to bow, to buy time, and even started to try and dip her head to the lion-women, but something inside her just wouldn't do it.

She breathed out, hard.

It was as if she was wired wrong. Maybe if she made a joke of it . . .

'Sorry. Bowing to gods. Not something us barbarians do very well . . .'

'THEN BE STILL!'

Stone hands grabbed her shoulders and plunged her beneath the flickering blue surface, holding her there until she stiffened and stopped moving, her face stretched wide in panic. Then they lifted her out and held her as the blue water slipped off her and fell back into the sarcophagus, leaving her uncannily as dry as if she hadn't been fully submerged at all.

She was dry, but she was now as unmoving as all the other people frozen in time.

The lion-woman holding her above the blue water looked a question at her sisters and the small cat standing between them.

'WE SHALL WAKE THE GIANT BEETLE. HAVE IT GUARD HER SOMEWHERE CLOSE

TO THE DOOR. WHERE SHE MAY BE SEEN BY THOSE WHO MAY SEEK HER.'

The cat turned away and jumped up onto the back of a smooth black stone sculpture the shape of a ladybird, but the size of a dining table. It began to vibrate beneath the cat's paws, as sharp legs unfolded from beneath its carapace and felt for the floor.

'SHE HAS LITTLE TO TELL US. SHE IS JUST MEAT. WE WILL SET AN AMBUSH WITH TWO DRAGONS HIDDEN IN FRONT OF THE BUILDING. SHE MAY DO BETTER BAITING A TRAP.'

14

The Supermarket Checkout

Little Tragedy was sitting on the step outside the supermarket trying to get over the horrible surprise of the cat's betrayal and the pain of the gash it had clawed on its cheek.

'I'm all right,' he kept on saying, smiling through the tears that were treacherously brimming in his eyes. Then, when it all got too much and he had to sob, he would snatch up the mask and put it in front of his face so the others couldn't see him cry. And then he would get himself together again, muster a smile and drop the mask until it all got too much again. Then he would repeat the cycle.

'He's in shock,' said the Fusilier. 'Be all right in a jiffy. And if he ain't, I'll carry him. We should be getting on and seeing to that arm of yours.'

Will looked at the bright lights of the supermarket behind them. The bright colours of the shelves were full of life, like a hint of the warm old world before it all froze and went grey with dusk, as it was out on the pavement. He felt thirsty, he felt hungry, and his arm, now the Fusilier drew his attention to it again, definitely still hurt.

He leant the dragon's shield against the window and stood up.

'I'll be back in a minute.'

'Where you going?' said Tragedy, his voice shaky from behind the mask.

'I'm going in there. There are pills that'll stop my arm hurting and I need a drink,' said Will.

'In and out,' said the Fusilier. 'Just get what you need. Know what you kids are like in a sweetie shop when no-one's looking. This ain't a jolly.'

Will slipped in the door past a woman with a double-wide buggy in which a pair of twins were stuck in the act of fighting over a juice-box, and then he was inside the supermarket, surrounded by bright light and vibrant colours. It felt like a kind of relief for his starved senses, though the silence was definitely unsettling.

The aisles were crammed with a rush-hour crowd of commuters stuck in the act of doing a quick shop on their way home: there was an old gent in a long, velvet-collared coat, there were young girls in short skirts and boots, two tubby men in turbans and beards, some skinny-jeaned hipsters with beards and no turbans, there were school-kids and pensioners, a one-legged man in a wheelchair and a long-legged girl on roller-skates. It was as mixed a crowd as London itself. Will couldn't help pushing the girl to see if the wheels on her boots would allow him to move her, but she remained as stuck as any of them.

He grinned. And then he felt her arm again. Gingerly, as if she might wake and shout at him at any moment, he reached up and touched her cheek to confirm what he'd felt when he pushed the arm. She was not warm. She was soft, as in made of flesh, but she didn't feel warm, not like his mother had. He wondered if every stuck person was slowly cooling down, and what that meant. Then he heard the memory of his dad's voice in his ear saying 'Trouble with you Will-o is that you think too much. Sometimes you just got to do!'

So he did: he pushed the nagging worry to the back of his head and got on with raiding the shelves.

He could have anything he liked. He could have stuff he wasn't allowed. He snagged a couple of cans of normally forbidden energy drink from the cold shelves and popped the tab on one while pocketing the other.

He chugged the sickly sweet and slightly medicinal fizz as he walked on up the confectionery aisle. The Fusilier was wrong: it was a 'jolly'. He shovelled packets of garishly coloured gummy sours into his pocket, and then rammed them home with a fistful of Mars bars. He left the empty can on a shelf while he struggled to zip his bulging pockets shut.

Then he opened the next can and chugged that one as he looked for the medicine aisle. He passed a cold cabinet full of sandwiches in triangular packs and stopped to grab a few of them; there were triple-decker all-day breakfast sandwiches that he was never allowed to have although he loved the cold sausage and bacon and egg filling. Out of pocket-space, he shoved them down inside his jacket which now bulged out so badly that he was starting to look like the world's most obvious shop-lifter.

Then he saw a rack of prawn mayonnaise sandwiches and felt a sudden pang of sadness: it was Jo's favourite filling. He took one and wodged it in with the others.

It was like a promise that he'd get to her and rescue her, somehow.

He was feeling a little better again when he heard a sudden rap on the glass at the front of the store. He peered down the long aisle and had just time to see The Fusilier pointing agitatedly up at the sky and then turn to him and hold up a hand in a gesture that clearly meant 'stay', and then draw his finger across his neck with a grimace that even more clearly meant 'danger'. The Fusilier grabbed the shield in one hand, Tragedy with the other, and ran out of sight.

And as simple as that Will was alone with nothing more than a jacket stuffed with sweets and sandwiches and a mouthful of all-day breakfast that suddenly tasted like mud.

Unsure what to do, or where to go, he kept his eyes fixed on the front of the store, because that's where whatever the danger was would most likely arrive. He edged slowly backwards, thinking he'd be safer out of the bright lights that only moments before had seemed so cheerful and full of life.

It's lucky he kept looking in that direction because he saw the cat a moment before it saw him, and was able to stop moving before it did.

He froze in the act of unconsciously pushing his jacket sleeve up his arm, his left hand on his right wrist. It was an awkward position, but in a way he was relieved at what he saw. He had thought from the urgency of the Fusilier's sign language that something more threatening than a bronze house-cat had appeared outside.

He wondered what it was about this cat, Hodge, that had put the fear into the two statues and made them run. The Fusilier had, after all, and without much worry, shot and killed a dragon, and dragons were much bigger and breathed fire. Maybe they still liked the cat despite it gashing Little Tragedy's cheek. He could understand that: no-one wants to shoot a cat, after all. Which just left a lingering question at the back of his mind: why had they looked so urgent about it? Then something stepped in behind the cat and answered that question horribly.

It was another dragon, its scales painted the same municipal silver as the others, its mouth the same angry red, its fangs just as large.

The cat raised a paw and scraped its claws down the window, making a horrible scree-ing noise that made Will's guts churn in fear. At least it felt like fear, but was also the effect of two highly carbonated cans of energy drink chugged at speed. Maybe that's why he suddenly felt nauseous.

The cat looked round at the dragon and the monster stepped closer to the window. The stone hawk Horus fluttered down to land between them, its blue-lit eyes scanning through the glass like little searchlights. Will thought there was something very familiar about it and its little pharaoh's cap, but before he could remember where he'd seen it the cat scree-ed its claws down the window again as if insisting, its eyes turning back to look right down the aisle Will was standing in. He hoped he looked indistinguishable from the other frozen people. He wanted to swallow, wanted to wet his suddenly dry mouth, but he didn't. He just stared back and fought the irresistible urge to blink.

The dragon's head peered from side to side above the insistent stare of the cat and the unblinking eye of Horus as the long neck snaked left and right, trying to make out what the cat was clearly wanting it to see.

Will didn't breathe.

The cat yowled, as if saying something to the dragon, and the dragon's mouth opened and let out a roar that shook the tins on the shelf next to Will. Horus shook his stone feathers and lofted off, back away into the night. Despite himself Will swallowed. The dragon didn't see it, because it strutted away from the window and tried to get in the door.

And here Will – much to his relief – noticed something Jo and he had first seen in the hospital when

Jo was happily stealing Smarties from the kid upending them into his mouth: the frozen people didn't move. Just as he had not been able to push the girl on roller-skates, the dragon seemed to be unable to move the woman with the double-wide buggy out of its way to make enough room to come inside the supermarket for a closer look at whatever the unpleasant cat was trying to draw its attention to.

Will allowed himself a shallow breath of relief. The normally immobile statues might be on the move, but the flip side of things – the world gone 'vicey-versey' as Tragedy had said – was that the normally mobile people, the 'Regulars' were as unmovable as the statues usually were.

That was going to save him.

It was a happy thought.

And it lasted for at least three seconds, right up until the dragon growled in frustration and gave up trying to fold its angular, wing-hobbled shape above, round or through the human barricade of the woman and her children and just stepped sideways and head-butted the glass window instead.

Just as Jo had been unable to move the kid in the bed, but had been able to steal some of his Smarties, so the Dragon was clearly able to move things if not people. And in this case the head-butt broke the window into smithereens of glass, hardened fragments that Will could hear being ground to powder beneath the dragon's metal talons as it stepped purposefully inside the shop.

Will would have run, but he didn't dare look behind him to see if there was anywhere to run to. He just stayed still and listened to his heart begin to trip-hammer while his mind raced furiously round and round in increasingly panicked circles trying to work out what to do.

The dragon crunched past the checkout lanes, and as it went, it carefully pushed at the unmoving people. At first Will thought it was doing it out of pure malice, like a drunk who bumps into people in a crowd on purpose, looking for a fight. Then he realized the dragon was just being methodical: if the people didn't move, they weren't what it was looking for. And he was pretty sure that when the dragon came to him, he would stumble and give himself away.

The dragon had a choice of three aisles to search. Will was in the middle one. It was quite crowded with frozen people. The two men in turbans made the kind of barrier he could see the dragon would not be able to squeeze past. Maybe that would save him. He saw the dragon turn into the aisle to his left and heard it snuffle and trudge its way along, its progress marked by little grunts as it shoved at what Will himself was beginning to think of as Regulars.

He tried to calm his shallow breathing as he heard the dragon draw level with him, on the other side of the shelves. There was a rattle and clatter of tinny wheel noise and a screech as the creature climbed over a trolley blocking its progress. Its wingtip smashed into the hanging light which began to swing wildly back and forth, strobing on and off, throwing crazed shadows dancing across the walls.

Will realized that the dragon would get to the top of the next-door aisle and come at him from behind. The two men in turbans would be of no use to him as a barricade.

He couldn't think of anything to do. He found his left hand was resting on the scarab bead on the bracelet round his right wrist. It seemed to have got hotter as the dragon got closer. He wondered if it could sense the dragon and was acting as a kind of warning device. Then he worried that the dragon might also be able to sense the stone. And as he worried even more about how painful and horrific things would get if the dragon *did* discover him he realized he did have one way out.

He could slip the bracelet off his wrist.

If his theory was right he would then be as frozen as any other Regular. It was a last choice, the kind of thing you do in despair. He wondered if it was just cowardice, a kind of suicide even. But surely this nightmare wouldn't go on forever? Surely the world would reboot and everything would go back to normal, and him with it? Taking the scarab off his wrist might not be a betrayal of Jo, of his mother?

And then, just as he was about to give up, he realized all hope was not quite lost. His one chance would be to wait until the dragon was committed to the aisle behind him, and then run for it. He could get past the two men in turbans, the dragon could not. The people jamming the aisles were a kind of maze for the large creature with its awkward wings and long spiny tail. It would have to double back and go down the other aisle to get after him. That might mean he could get out into the street, and have at least a chance of getting away. He wouldn't have to give up!

He steeled himself not to move as he tracked the dragon's progress by sound alone. The strobing light swinging back and forth made everything seem even more frightening and disorienting and so he closed his eyes. It helped him concentrate on the sound. He heard it scrabble and grunt some more, and then the sound of its talons dragging across the tiled floor got clearer and he realized it was now approaching him from behind. In Will's memory there were only a couple of people between him and the back of the shop, but he wasn't sure. It had just been an impression and he hadn't focused on it, largely because he had had no idea his life would depend on the information. He decided to wait until he heard two grunts as the dragon pushed people and then sprint for it.

And then his stomach rumbled. Loudly, rudely and disastrously. All the fizzy sugary energy drink had betrayed him. The dragon stopped dead. He could hear it listening.

And worse than that, he could feel a ball of fizzy gas trying to force its way back up his windpipe in what was going to be a colossal burp. He tried to block his throat. He clenched his teeth tight shut, locking his jaw. He tried to swallow the burp back down. But it was no good. He was going to burp or burst.

He would have to run for it.

And as he opened his eyes two really bad things happened at once. He saw Hodge the cat perched on the shoulder of one of the turbaned men, waiting for him, its tail flicking mockingly back and forward, and

146

he felt the wet heat of the dragon's breath and the heavy, slimy weight of its tongue sliding round his neck. He bunched every muscle in his body, ready to resist the dragon's coming shove, but it never came.

The dragon made a grunt like a nasty chuckle and slid a talon gently down his back, slitting the jacket clean as a razor. It knew. A cascade of wrapped sandwiches fell about his feet. The cat stared at him. He felt his eyeballs drying out as he tried not to blink. He felt his lungs begin to scream for air.

All they had to do was wait for him to breath or belch or blink and he was done. He heard the dragon's scales slither as it drew back it arm to shove him, and in the momentary blackness of the strobing light he did the only thing he could do.

He said sorry in his head and slid the scarab bracelet off in one tiny, very fast movement of his hand.

He didn't even have time to realize he was right about the scarab and what would happen if he took it off .

His world stopped. He saw nothing, not even black.

He felt nothing, thought nothing, was nothing.

It was over.

He was done.

15

The Prudential Angels

And then he wasn't.

His vision kicked back in and everything was different. The swinging light had stopped swinging, there was no hot tongue round his neck, and he couldn't see the nasty cat because the Fusilier's blurred face filled his field of vision, too close to focus on. Something was tugging at his hand.

'There you are,' grinned the Fusilier and stepped back. Will looked down to see Little Tragedy pushing the scarab bracelet back onto his wrist.

Will felt swoony and sick, but still had enough energy to spin round and see what had happened to the Dragon.

The shop seemed to have experienced a small explosion in the toilet tissue aisle.

'It's gone,' said Tragedy proudly. 'We was in that bus over the street. Fusilier had his gun on the Dragon and was about to shoot it when you just went still.'

'Bloody thing, thought it had you bang to rights,' said the Fusilier. 'Truth is it did, 'cos it was going to be a tricky one. Didn't have a clear shot and with all that swinging light I was as likely to drill you as it. Then it tried to shove you.'

'Tried to shove you so hard that when you didn't move it fell backwards,' laughed Tragedy. 'Ho! It didn't expect that, did it? Fell right into all those packs of paper streamers and got itself into a right old how'd you do!'

'Stormed back into the street festooned in bog paper,' said the Fusilier. 'Very cheesed off it was. Grabbed poor old Hodge by the tail and tossed him over the roof opposite. Howled like a screaming firework, that cat did!'

'Serves him right,' said Tragedy, feeling the gashes on his cheek. 'Maybe it'll knock some normal back into him. What's bog paper?'

The Fusilier exchanged a look with Will.

'Not something you need ever worry about,' he said. 'Not an issue for us lot. Now Will boy, we should get going.'

Will slumped against the shelves and felt his arm. It was throbbing again. And though he still felt sick, it was a different kind of sick to being sick with fear.

This was being sick with relief. He'd survived. He could still rescue Jo. He looked down at the sandwich packets round their feet. He bent and picked one up. The Prawn Mayonnaise.

'This is all I need,' he said. 'That and some paracetamol.'

'What's parrots-eat-'em-all?' said Little Tragedy.

'It's why there aren't any aspirin in the jungle,' said Will.

Little Tragedy crinkled his brow and looked at the Fusilier who shrugged.

'It's a joke,' said Will. 'Just the wrong way round.'

'Must be a Regular thing,' said the Fusilier with another shrug.

'Like bog paper?' said Tragedy.

'You really don't want to know,' said the Fusilier. 'Trust me.'

Two minutes and a couple of painkillers later, they were back on the street and jogging through the frozen commuters scattered across their pathway like an obstacle course. Will felt lighter and stronger. They'd retrieved the dragon shield and Tragedy was helping him carry it, but in truth the longer he held it the better he felt, as if it were somehow charging his battery.

'Here,' he said. 'I can take it now. I feel better.'

'That parrots-eat-'em-all must be magic stuff,' said Tragedy, looking a little let down as he relinquished his grip on the shield. Will realized he really did like being part of something, like the little kid who always wants to play with the older ones. He remembered being that kid. He remembered Jo being that kid too.

'Not them,' said Will. 'I think it's the shield. Don't know why. Thanks for the help, Tradge. Couldn't have managed without you.'

Tragedy beamed proudly.

'Maybe we can ask at the meeting,' he said.

'The Tithing?' said Will, remembering Victory's words. 'What's this Tithing this all about, anyway?'

'It's just a get-together. Of Spits. Like a parliament of statues sort of thingy, if you like. When something goes . . . odd like this we all get together at the Ghost Church and discuss what's to be done and who should do it.'

'Ghost Church?' said Will. 'That doesn't sound very good . . .'

'Just a name,' said the Fusilier, curtly. 'Names can't hurt you. Not paying attention can. So keep up and stop asking questions.'

He jogged ahead. He jogged onwards, threading

through the dark forest of pedestrians stuck on the pavement. Tragedy ran a little closer to Will and spoke quietly.

'I been thinking: come midnight, if that dragon you took the shield from gets popped back on its plinth by the other dragons, maybe it'll come looking for it. Might be more dangerous than safe, see. Dragon'd be able to sense where it is and come for it. Come for you.'

'Maybe I'll swap it then,' said Will, with more bravado in his voice than he actually felt. 'Maybe it can have its shield back if they give me my sister.'

'And maybe worms can juggle,' snorted the Fusilier. 'Dragons don't work like that. Least not the silver ones. Silver ones are stupid, all made from the same dull mould. The old Temple Bar Dragon, on the other hand, is a whole different kettle of fish.'

'Or lizards,' grinned Tragedy, looking up at Will. 'Kettle of lizards. 'Cos it's a dragon. That's a joke'.

'Yes,' said Will. 'That's a good one.'

He was about to ask what the Temple Bar Dragon was like, but the Fusilier accelerated and he needed all his spare breath to keep going.

They followed him along the wide street called Holborn, then he suddenly disappeared.

It took Will a moment to realize that he had turned sharp left and run under the arch of a red-brick building that looked like the architect couldn't choose between designing a castle or a cathedral, and so had decided to build both at once. Will followed the Fusilier through the arch and slowed suddenly.

This was a place where some of the outside lights had clearly been on when time froze, because the space he was now in was glowing like hot coals: uplighters splashed deep orangey red illumination on the brick vaulted ceiling of the cloister he was standing below. It should have been a warm and welcoming glow in the heart of the largely dark city, but Will found it unsettling.

He slowly followed the Fusilier across a small open space and under a much wider arch into the second, central courtyard. They had to wind their way through a party of Japanese tourists frozen in the act of listening to a tour-guide, who was pointing at the glowing dome poking up through the ground, as if someone had made a glass replica of St Paul's Cathedral beneath them and jammed the roof up through the paving stones. It too was lit from below and surrounded with a base of shiny pink granite and black stone, like a giant snow globe. It threw light on the surrounding high walls and gothic windows that now penned them in. Like anything lit strongly from underneath, it looked dramatic and sinister, and just a bit infernal.

Because the great dome was so bright it took him a moment to see who the Fusilier had started talking to, but as he stepped forward he saw that there was a huge war memorial jammed in the corner, and it was with the bronze angels on top of it that he was speaking. There were two of them, and they had huge wildly overcomplicated wings stretched above them as they cradled the body of a dead soldier who they were regarding with looks of the most heartrending sadness.

They perched on top of a tall and impressive plinth which had bronze statues of young nymphs holding funeral wreaths at all four corners.

'Need a spot of help,' said the Fusilier to the angels. 'Got a boy here with a hurt arm.'

'That's right,' piped Tragedy. 'Could do with some ministering.'

The angels looked at him. They didn't say anything, but their wings – which definitely looked too much for just two of them – shifted, and the light robes they wore riffled in their own invisible breeze in a way that reminded Will of Ariel's. Then they looked away, back down at the dead soldier, as if dismissing the Fusilier.

Will's arm throbbed badly again. The running had made the blood pound round him and the paracetamol weren't very strong. He sat down on the stone bench round the dome and got his breath.

He looked to his right and saw there was another pair of smaller war memorials, like bronze noticeboards facing each other on either side of a second entrance to the courtyard. On top of them, two knights were standing with lances from which bronze pennants fluttered. They had no helmets and looked more like modern soldiers than mediaeval knights. In fact they looked like a couple of clean cut young men about town, the kind he'd seen in the old black and white films his dad liked to watch, a couple of dandies who had dressed up in the armour as a spot of fancy dress fun.

They were also only three feet tall, but nevertheless they were leaning forward and looking at him.

Statues moving around was one thing when they were human sized or even when they were bigger than he was – his shocked brain had begun to get used to that – but there was something about these miniature humans that added an extra layer of strange to everything.

'By George, George!' said one to the other. 'It's a boy. And he isn't frozen like the others.'

'You're right George,' the other replied. 'Deuced odd, if you ask me.'

They both sounded very old fashioned and rather posh.

'Maybe we should ask him,' said the first. 'Looks like a decent enough chap . . .'

Will couldn't really cope with extra strange right now, so he turned away from them before they spoke to him and looked at the Fusilier instead. At least he was close to normal size.

'Why aren't they helping?' he said to the Fusilier. 'You said that the angels would help.'

'Oh, you don't want *their* help,' said a gentle girl's voice. 'Not theirs, my word, no you don't . . .'

He looked up to see that one of the nymphs had stepped off the plinth and was walking towards him, so light-footed that she seemed to waft an inch above the shiny pavement. Before he could say that actually he *did* want help, because his arm was getting more and more painful by the second she smiled and reached out a hand.

156

'Come,' she said. 'These two angels are in charge of easing the passage from life. You can see just by looking at them that they're sad angels of Passing, plain as a pikestaff. Same as I can see you're too young to be needing that kind of help right now. Your wound is not going to kill you . . .'

She led him round the back of the memorial where the mystery of the complicated wings was revealed: what had looked from the front as if the sculptor had not known when to stop adding feathers was in fact the back view of the wings of a third, hidden angel who sat behind the other two, facing the corner. She was not cradling a corpse, but was instead holding a small baby.

'She's for Life, you see?' said the nymph, pushing him forward encouragingly.

As if in response to her words the baby gave a happy shriek of delight, followed by a gurgling laugh that echoed around the four walls and for a moment made everything seem better, as if all was well with the world.

The angel looked up from the baby's face and smiled at him.

'You're in pain, my child,' she said.

Will felt a thick knot rise in his throat at her words. It made him unable to speak without choking on it, so he just nodded mutely and concentrated on keeping his eyes dry.

He was surprised to find that there were suddenly tears lurking there, and he didn't want to be seen letting them out.

It wasn't what she said.

It was the voice she said it in.

It was so exactly like his mother's voice that it made the hair rise on the back of his neck. It also made him feel like a little child, something he had not been for a very long time.

The angel stepped off the plinth and handed the gurgling bronze baby to the waiting nymph. She rolled up her sleeves and came and knelt in front of him. Her hands, which were much softer and warmer than he would have expected, reached out and held his head, gently touching his cheeks. Her eyes peered into his. He could not look away, nor did he really want to. They were full of warmth and understanding, and he could see crinkles at the edges as she smiled at him.

'You're hurt,' she said.

'My arm,' he replied.

'Your arm I can fix,' she said. 'But that's just physical pain. It will do you no lasting damage. What's really hurting you is inside, and only you can heal that.'

Her hand dropped to his burned arm and he felt the throbbing pain leech out, to be replaced by nothing more than a gentle warmth.

Now his arm was not troubling him, he felt all the other things that were: he felt tired and frightened and hungry and thirsty and most of all, *worst* of all, stuck and powerless. He felt powerless because he didn't understand any of this. It was too big. And he was too small.

'My child,' said the angel and pulled him close to her, folding her arms and wings around him. 'Don't worry. You are stronger than you think.'

'What's inside me?' he whispered. 'Is it why this is happening to me?'

He felt her laugh as much as heard it, a gentle rumble against his cheek.

'No child. What's hurting you is what you think about yourself. Only you can change that. This frozen city is bigger than you. This is old power, dark power. It is a wrongness being worked upon London and because of it the city has fallen out of time. You are just trapped in it.'

'So it's not my fault?'

'No. Not yours. Though who knows? The righting of it might be. Nothing that happens happens without

159

an effect. The world, as you have found out, is stranger than most Regulars notice.'

'What about the hurt inside me?' he said, his voice thick and scratchy. 'What is that?'

'That you can heal,' she said and squeezed him. 'I told you that. What it is I cannot tell, for it is not my gift to see all your secrets, but it is my place to see a good heart and to give it hope and knowledge of its own strength. And maybe if you can heal you—'

She never finished, because instead of fate dealing what Will felt sure was about to be the final piece of a very important puzzle, it dealt dragons, and it dealt a full hand of them.

All at once.

The dragons who came this time were not like the ones that Will had seen before. There were more of them – four or five in all, though in the confusion of the fight that followed it was hard to see exactly how many. But most importantly they were smaller than the other ones.

As far as he could see in the infernal glow of the courtyard, they were exactly the same silver-painted dragons with the red lolling tongues, but they were only waist high.

And being smaller, they moved much, much faster.

At least two came over the roofs and dropped in on either side of the Fusilier, trails of wildfire pluming out of their nostrils and marking their descent like plummeting fireworks, and two more came through the main arch with a vicious turn of speed, talons scrabbling on the polished granite beneath.

And they clearly came prepared, not just because they had built up the flames inside their throats and were ready to spit fire as soon as they found a target, but because they had a plan, which was for them all to attack the Fusilier first.

16

Georges and Dragons

It was a good plan.

It was also fuelled by vengeance because the Fusilier had shot their brother dragon when rescuing Will back at the playground. Maybe that desire for revenge made their attack all the more savage. Maybe they would have done so anyway.

Whatever the reason, it happened so fast, and so brutally that Will couldn't begin to move. It wasn't even fear that froze him. It was pure shock. His mind just didn't have time to catch up fast enough to think what his body should be doing.

The dragons that flamed in out of the dark sky landed on either side of the Fusilier with a colossal crash of metal on stone, shrieking streams of wildfire right at him. Shriek was the word. Where the larger dragons had roared as they attacked, in this case the spiralling jets of flame were accompanied by a high scream pitched so high and loud that the one thing Will's body *did* do was slap its hands over its ears to stop the vicious sound needling into his brain.

The Fusilier managed to get his rifle off his shoulder, but as he tried to aim it at the dragon in front of him one of the other dragons leapt up onto his shoulder and chunked its fangs deep into his neck.

Metal sparked on metal as the teeth bit in and the creature worried at him like a terrier. As he tried to throw it off, another dragon shot its own jet of wildfire into his body.

The Fusilier staggered to keep on his feet, his torso wreathed in twining ropes of flame.

His eyes found Will.

'Run!' he shouted, his mouth gaping wide. 'Run bo—'

The small dragon on his shoulder wrenched its fangs out of his neck and snaked its head round to fire a concentrated jet of fire right into his shouting mouth at point blank range.

Little Tragedy yelped in horror and ran away into the darkness.

The angel that had been holding Will whirled and scooped the nymph and the baby inside the protection

of its arms and then, with a powerful beat of its wings that sounded like a thunderclap, lofted them all into the sky, away from the fire splashing across the courtyard floor.

She hung there, twenty feet above the dragons, each beat of her wings winnowing the flames flat against the stone in the downdraft, far enough for immediate safety, but close enough for Will to have a perfect view of The Fusilier's fate . . . and what followed.

The Fusilier choked and stumbled, but the dragon held onto his neck, and one by one – horribly – the other dragons adjusted their aim so that the soldier was suddenly stuck in a kind of crouch, halfway to falling over as four jets of wildfire converged to a white hot point between his teeth. He gagged and jerked and then with a ghastly cough swallowed once. His neck melted and his head fell back, all the way back, so it was hanging down between his shoulder blades like a gruesome backpack, and he was still.

Will heard himself shouting 'No!' at the horror of it all, and then something ran beneath him and hit one of the dragons in the side.

The dragon choked off its fire-stream and looked round, snarling in surprise. One of the small bare-headed knights from the side entrance had run it through with his lance.

The small dragon now found itself fighting a human of the same scale. It was as small as him, but it was also as fast.

It tried to bite the knight, but the knight used the lance like a lever and threw the dragon across the courtyard, letting go of the shaft like a hammer thrower, so that it hit another dragon and knocked it flying. As those two dragons tried to untangle their wings and lashing tails and get back on their feet, he just kept on coming, his hand disappearing under his long chainmail coat and emerging with a broadsword clenched in his fist.

He leapt fearlessly at the tangled dragons, springing across the wildfire splashing over the paving stones, sword swinging in a merciless double-handed arc.

The dragons raised their heads just in time to meet the blade neck first. The heavy sword barely noticed passing through one neck, and kept on going right through the second. The knight skidded to a halt just in front of the two dragon's briefly surprised – and now suddenly dead and headless – bodies, the momentum of his swing spinning him round, so that he ended up facing back towards Will and the other dragons.

Almost in slow-motion the two heads of the dragons he had just decapitated dropped to the ground on either side of him and bounced to a standstill.

He didn't even bother to look back at them.

Instead he sheathed his sword in one smooth move, dropped his freed hand, and found the haft of the spear still impaling the dragon.

He jerked it free, and charged the remaining dragons, reversing it pointy-end forward as he ran.

The first dragon spun to face him, and had enough time to put its shield up to protect itself.

Unfortunately for it, the other knight hurtled out of the flames to its side, chopping his sword downwards like an axe.

To give it its due, the dragon did – technically – keep hold of the shield but the talon that gripped it was cleanly sheared from its arm, so the shield dropped forward just in time to allow the incoming spear point to impale it in the centre of the chest. The second knight hurdled the spear handle and ran at the next dragon, sword arm already cocked for another blow.

The dragons had used surprise and speed to gain the first advantage. They had not expected a counter-attack, and certainly not one delivered so fast and so expertly.

The dragon spat fire at the incoming knight.

Will thought that was going to be the end of him, but instead the knight swung his sword straight in front of himself, holding it like an altar-boy holds a candle, and calmly charged ahead.

The sword's blade split the wildfire so that it passed on either side of him.

The dragon's eyes bulged in surprise and it redoubled the strength of the fire stream. But the knight gritted his teeth and leaned in, as if pushing his way relentlessly forward against a mighty wind.

He pushed in step-by-step until he was nose-to-nose with the dragon who now had to use its shield to stop his progress and try to shove him away.

The knight reached back calmly with one open hand.

'Trouble you for your lance, old boy?' he said, cool as a surgeon asking a nurse for a scalpel. The other knight yanked the spear out of the previous dragon and threw it underhand across the courtyard towards him.

It slapped into his hand, which closed with a sharp snap.

The dragon just turned and ran.

Its wings whirred behind it as it stumbled its

panic-stricken way into the sky, climbing desperately for safety.

The knight sheathed his sword and hefted the spear with a rather disappointed look as he watched the dragon attain the height of the rooftops.

'Two bob says you can't, George,' said his companion, sounding rather cheerful and not at all like a mediaeval knight ought to.

The dragon disappeared into the gloom above with a final silvery flash of wings and a distant shriek of defiance.

The one with the lance reached back like a javelin thrower and hurled it high into the darkness. He turned and grinned at his partner.

'When did you ever have two bob, George?' he said.

There was a thump and a squawk from the darkness above.

Both the St Georges squinted up into the night.

At first there was nothing, then there was a second squawk, and then a frenzied spiral of silvery wings and lashing tail as the dragon whirled out of the sky like a downed helicopter.

The first St George stepped calmly sideways and let the lifeless body slam into the paving stone he had just vacated. He looked at the ruin of the crash, casting a cool eye on the smoking debris.

'Hmm,' he said. 'Golly. That's two bob you owe me there.'

The other St George stepped over and plucked the lance out of the wrecked dragon. He looked at it with visible disapproval. It was definitely now L-shaped.

'You bent my bally lance, you clumsy blighter! It's going to be the devil of a job to get it straight again.'

'Wait until midnight, old bean,' said his companion 'Midnight heals all.'

'Midnight's a way off,' said the angel, dropping back to the ground. 'There will be more mayhem before then. And this boy needs our help.'

Tragedy, now he could see the danger was gone, slipped out from behind a pillar and wiped his nose, sniffing away his tears as if they had never been there.

The Georges and the angels stood around the broken body of the Fusilier while Will told them everything that he knew about what was happening. Which was not, he realized as he spoke, much.

Then the talk turned to what to do next, the first thing being to deal with the Fusilier before midnight so he could regenerate and be free of his wounds.

'It may not be a midnight as we have known

midnights to be,' said one of the angels hesitantly. 'It may be a dead midnight . . .'

Will didn't like the sound of a dead midnight.

'And with no true midnight those who are stuck or dead will stay as our friend the Fusilier here,' said one of the mourning angels.

He could see from the looks that the Georges exchanged that they didn't like this talk either.

'Oh put a sock in it, old misery-guts,' said one of them with a cheery grin. He clearly didn't have a lot of reverence for the angel, who in her turn bristled visibly.

'That's no way to speak to an angel,' she said.

'And don't be so hoity-toity,' he grinned.

'Or so jolly gloomy,' said the other George. 'Very sapping to the old morale and all that bunk. Now, chop chop, the three of you get the poor old Fusilier here back on his plinth, and we'll cut along to the meeting at the Ghost Church and take our new friend Will here with us.'

Will still thought the Ghost Church sounded pretty gloomy too, but decided now wasn't the time to mention it. The other George pointed at Little Tragedy.

'You coming too, young Tradge? Ghost Church,

double-time. Hooky'll want to know why he ain't stopped like the other Regulars.'

17

Hooky and the Ghost Church

Putting The Fusilier back on his plinth didn't take too long, since it stood in the middle of Holborn at the junction of Grays Inn Road, not far from where they were.

The three angels lifted him between them and flew him back out onto the dark street and down to where he usually stood. Will and Little Tragedy watched, eyes searching the sky for movement, in case more dragons came.

'Don't worry about the dragons,' said a voice from below. He looked down to see the two small knights standing next to him.

'George is right,' said the other. 'They're unlikely to be stupid enough to attack you with a couple of likely lads like us travelling with you.'

'Thank you, George,' said the other. 'Let's get cracking then.'

And with that they led off into the street, threading

their way through the frozen pedestrians and eventually finding a strip of clearer road along the central divider in the middle of the street, between the unmoving slabs of buses and cars.

'Are you both called George?' asked Will as they hurried along.

It was strange talking to these mini people as if they were normal.

'Course we are, old bean,' said the first. 'Saint Georges really. Though George here and I don't feel particularly saintly, to tell the truth. Bit of a disappointment to all the other Georges in that way I expect . . .'

'There are lots of us dotted about the old metrop,' said the second George, with a cheery smile. 'Just as many of us as there are dragons, more or less.'

'Old London saying,' said Little Tragedy, 'for every George there's a dragon.'

'Means for every solution there's a problem,' said the first George. 'Or should that be the other way round? For every problem, there's a solution? Yes. Sounds better.'

'And that's us,' said the other one, cheerfully. 'Solutions.'

'Lucky for you,' said Tragedy. 'Know a thing or two

about dragon-slaying do the Georges . . .'

'I saw that,' said Will. 'Thank you.'

'All in a day's work,' smiled the one with the lance.

'It's just our job,' said the other.

'And who's this Hooky we're going to see?' said Will.

'Duke of Wellington. He's normally on a plinth outside the Royal Exchange. Military genius but a bit of a bully, so you know the drill, just look him in the eye and push back at him. He'll back off and respect you for it.'

'Absolutely,' said the other. 'That or have you tied to a gun carriage and given fifty lashes.'

Will didn't like the sound of that, but he did feel safer moving through the time-stopped city with three companions, even if two of them were half-sized. Their cheery personalities seemed to make up for their lack of inches.

He felt in his pocket. Jo's bracelet was there, and the sandwich he was saving was in the other one. The jacket was a bit useless since the dragon at the supermarket had ripped it down the back, but he kept it on for now. He looked at the frozen people they were jogging past and thought he might find someone his size and borrow their coat if he had time, but right

175

now he needed to keep up.

As they turned down King Edward Street they met a statue of a warhorse topped by a knight. It stood in the middle of the road in a way that reminded Will of the mounted policemen he'd seen with his dad when going to football matches. Remembering his dad jerked him out of the now he was trapped in with a pang of dangerously sharp nostalgia; it made him realize he was getting perilously used to this bad-dream London with its frozen people and moving statues. He was getting so used to it that the normal world was already drifting away in his mind, like an island slowly heading for the horizon as he travelled in the opposite direction, an island he might never return to.

He felt sick at the thought.

The Knight – another St George, this one from Regent's Park, as Tragedy helpfully told him – waved them on.

'Pass friends,' he rumbled through his visor, and turned back to his sentry duty.

They turned the next corner and Will looked up. His first thought was that the great dome of St Paul's Cathedral suddenly hanging above them must be the Ghost Church: it made sense. It was the biggest and most prestigious church in the city. But he couldn't understand why the great crowd of statues he found himself approaching wasn't going inside.

It was an extraordinary sight, and he stopped, even as the small Georges carried on greeting old friends – some mounted, most not – amongst the throng of metal and stone statues loitering in the street in between the unmoving City workers, a crowd that spilled across the pavement into a small park.

The mass of spits contained characters from all of London's long history. He saw a Roman soldier talking to a pair of Guardsmen in tall bearskins, and a caped nurse with a severe face telling off a king in a long curly wig. There was a bunch of soldiers like The Fusilier in rounded tin helmets that mirrored the dome above them, and they clustered together, but mainly the effect was of a great mixture: kings, politicians, explorers, nymphs, writers and at least two Peter Pans flitting about between them all.

'Why don't they go in?' he said to Little Tragedy, pointing at St Paul's.

'Oh. That's not the Ghost Church, silly,' said the boy. He pointed behind Will. 'That is. Was a real church before it was flattened in the last war. Will be again. Once the Firemen arrive. You'll see. It's a right laugh watching them build it. Like fireworks but with

177

hoses . . .'

Will turned and looked at the city park area behind him. It looked like it had been jammed in between towering buildings in much the same way the recreation area where Jo had been taken was, but then he realized that the tall spire and the side wall were the derelict ruin of a church, and what he had taken to be a park was in fact laid out inside what would have been the nave. As his eyes adjusted he saw there were regularly spaced wooden trellises in the shape of square columns with creepers climbing up them where the old stone pillars of the church would have run down either side of the aisle.

Before he could ask another question there was a sudden commotion as three more tin-helmeted figures pushed through the crowd with shouts of, 'Mind your backs!' and 'Coming through!'.

They looked like they were made of soot-blackened metal, and wore long double-breasted jackets with buttons running down each side of their chests. As they ran they carried a powerful looking fire-hose which they then unrolled and, with quick and practised movements, attached to a hydrant set into the pavement.

Two of them braced themselves holding the nozzle

of the hose and the third turned the tap. The hose sprung into life, like a great snake. The firemen bunched their muscles and directed the vigorous jet of water in a long arc up and over the park.

At first Will thought the Spits below were going to be pretty angry at getting such a hefty soaking, but then he saw the water slam into the back wall of the spire in a great splash of white spray, and instead of seeing it fall straight back to the ground under control of normal gravity, he saw the Ghost Church take shape.

The water did not drop vertically, at least not at first, and not in the way he expected: it flowed sideways as it pooled and spread down on either side of an invisible roof across the park, dripping and curling along and down the contours of the old church roof, and the walls and buttresses that had once stood there. The water licked around the outline like wet flames, casting a pale green light across the crowd assembled beneath. Will saw the empty trellises fill up with water and continue upwards to meet the newly revealed roof, and branching sideways to fill up the outline of a first-floor gallery that ran the length of the nave. Windows appeared, as did the unmistakable shape of a massive pipe organ at one end.

As the firemen jacked off the water, and the flow stopped abruptly, the old church stood there in all its former glory, everything that been destroyed by fire now re-made of standing water that swirled and flowed as if it was alive.

Will thought he'd never seen anything so beautiful. He was about to say so, when a shadow fell across him and a commanding voice snapped out over the heads of the crowd.

'Will someone sort out this rabble! This is meant to be a serious meeting not a monkey's tea party!'

A man on a horse, in tight britches, and a cocked hat looked down at him, along a nose like the beak of an angry bird. Somehow Will did not need to be told that this was Hooky, the Duke of Wellington. There can't have been two noses in London like that.

'That's a Regular!' the Duke said. 'That's not a Spit, by god. The devil is he doing here when all other Regulars are stuck?'

'He's got—' began Tragedy, but Will trod on his foot.

He thought it might be a good idea to keep the secret about the scarab bead to himself. There was something so severe about the Duke that it made Will think he might just decide to simplify things by taking the scarab and turning him off like a switch.

'. . . er he's got no . . . idea,' said Tragedy. 'Not clear yet.'

'Hmm,' said the Duke. 'A most irregular Regular. Don't like it. Keep out of the way, you too little imp. This is no place for children. We have a crisis to handle here.'

'I'm not a child . . .' said Will, but he was speaking to the Duke's back. He'd been dismissed.

18

The Meeting

The spits who were outside the Ghost Church filed in to join the others, and Will and Little Tragedy were caught up in the flow. They found a place about halfway back on a park bench, from where they watched the proceedings. The Duke rode his horse to the end of the church and turned to look at the assembled crowd.

'Right,' he barked. 'Stand easy and listen up.'

'Why's he in charge?' said Will. 'I mean he's a Duke and all but there are some other people wearing crowns in here.'

'Just is,' said Tragedy. 'Greatest General ever they says. The Iron Duke!'

'Leadership is not about titles, youngster ,' said a voice from about knee level. He looked down to see the two Georges grinning up at them. 'It's about force of personality, and he is the big cheese because no one else has had the bally nerve to tell him he isn't.'

The Duke may have been in charge, but it was clear once he began talking that all the other Spits wanted to chip in and add their thoughts. Within a couple of minutes it had turned into a barely controlled shouting match, with the Duke as referee.

The talk kept circling around the fact that time stopping had happened before, but that it had never lasted this long, and it was going on longer than before, what did it mean? And why were the dragons attacking when they should be defending the city? Some spits said the dragons had gone mad, some said they were under some kind of spell.

Will gathered from the casual way they all talked about magic that there was quite a long history of magic going wrong in the city, because they didn't seem especially surprised by it all. The problem was that none of them had any idea where the magic might be coming from, and if they did not get time back into joint before midnight it was also possible that Spits like Ariel and the Fusilier would not be regenerated and would be frozen for ever. Which gave him a horrible premonition about his mother and Jo.

The general feeling was that they would eventually find out who was behind this and shut them down, but that London was too vast a haystack to find the needle in with anything like enough speed to avoid very serious damage.

Will looked around the watery building and felt his frustration building. Too much talking, none of which really was helping, none of which he really understood, and certainly none of which was helping him get Jo or his mother moving again.

'This is ridiculous!' he said to Tragedy. 'It's all talk. Nothing's getting done. This is all—'

Will had the uncomfortable feeling that everything had gone a little too quiet and that everyone was now listening to them. He looked up and saw the Duke glaring.

'If the boy has *quite* finished talking?' he said with icy politeness.

'His name is Will,' said the Georges in unison.

'His name is not of great interest to me,' said the Duke, 'but his situation is. I am reminded that we have not yet established why he alone moves when all the Regulars don't.'

Everyone turned to look at Will with interest. He felt suddenly very alone and uncomfortable under this mass scrutiny. The Duke pointed at Tragedy.

'Little Tragedy. Is he otherly gifted? A Maker, a

Shifter, or even some hitherto unseen species of boy-Glint?'

'No, your grace,' said Tragedy. 'He's a perfectly normal boy just like me. Standard issue. He's worried about his sister though. He's a good egg.'

'Are you, Mr Will?' said the Duke. 'A good egg?'

'I don't know,' said Will.

'Well, what else DO you know? Do you for example know why or how time has stopped in the city?' said the Duke.

Will shook his head.

'Do you know who has stopped it?'

Again Will shook his head. The Duke sighed with disappointment and cleared his throat.

'Then if you have none of those pieces of information, perhaps you would do us the great favour of sitting quietly back there and letting your elders and betters try and solve this problem before it gets out of hand.'

'OK,' said Will, 'I don't know why, or how or who. But when you want to know *where* I think all this is coming from, let me know. I mean if you want to find the needle in that haystack you're all talking about.'

The Duke blinked and watched him sit down.

'Right' he said. 'I'll bite. Stand up and say your

piece. You have my attention.'

'Good,' said Will, staying in the sitting position. 'And now I'd like your word.'

'Careful,' said Tragedy under his breath. 'Old Hooky has a temper.'

'And why would I give my word to an insolent puppy?' said the Duke.

'Because if I'm right, I need your help,' said Will. 'If I can help you find out who's doing this by telling you where I think it's coming from, then I'd like you to do something for me.'

'Very mercenary,' said the Duke. 'Rather distasteful. Not a gentleman's attitude.'

'I just want you to help get my sister back,' said Will. 'That's all.'

'Oh!' said the Duke, and harrumphed.

Will had never actually heard anyone harrumph before: it was an embarrassed clearing of the throat mixed in with a cough and a grunt.

'Is that all?' said the Duke. 'Well. Apologies. Does you credit, I'm sure. And I've no doubt we should have done that anyway in the normal course of things, once this is over. But yes . . .'

He looked round the phalanx of soldiers in front of him. All the heads nodded.

'. . . we will of course help a lady in distress.'

Will decided not to say she wasn't a lady, she was only a Jo, a very annoying and often quite rude sort of a sister, but he decided not to.

'OK,' he said, fishing in his pocket and pulling out Jo's broken bracelet. 'If there's magic behind this, then whatever stops the magic must be the same kind of magic, don't you think?'

'Maybe,' said the Duke.

Will held out the bracelet.

'You know what that is?'

'A bead?' said the Duke.

'A coffee bean,' said one of the Georges.

'It's an Egyptian beetle,' said Will. 'It's called a scarab.'

The Duke looked at Will.

'I know what it is because there's a huge one in the British Museum. My mum took me there. There's a whole room, in fact there's lots of huge rooms full of Egyptian stuff. And when my sister was wearing this, she wasn't affected by the magic. She moved like me. Then when it was torn off she stopped like everyone else. So it must be Egyptian magic, and if it is, then the first place you should look is in the British Museum.'

'How do you know the beetle works?' said the

Duke. 'Do you have a beetle?'

'Scarab,' said Will and held up his wrist. 'And yes.'

'And your sister was taken?' said the Duke.

'I just told you: she froze the moment the bead broke off her wrist,' said Will. 'I saw it. It was horrible. And then I had to slip it off my wrist to avoid getting taken by another dragon, and I froze until Tradge here put it back on for me.'

'I did,' said Tragedy proudly, looking round at the crowd. 'I did! Me! He was froze and then I brought him back to life!'

'That proves it was the bead,' said George. 'And the bead says it's ancient Egyptian magic. There was also a stone hawk that looked very Egyptian that was with the cat Hodge, and the place where there's most Ancient Egyptian stuff is . . .'

'As you say, in the museum,' finished the Duke. 'Good thinking. Not final proof by any means but . . .'

He raised a hand to stop Will's objection.

'. . . but, by an embarrassingly long chalk, the very best idea we've had so far. Right, volunteers. I want a scouting party. . . .'

The Duke might have been a stiff-necked snob when running a meeting, but once he had a plan to make, Will could see he was something else entirely.

All the other spits stopped arguing or trying to have their say and just listened to him. In a few clear and short sentences he had outlined what he wanted, who should 'volunteer' and how they should proceed.

The only problem was that none of the planning seemed to involve Will being part of the group.

'Excuse me,' he said.

No one heard. So he shouted.

'EXCUSE ME!'

Everyone stopped and turned to look at him again.

'I'm going too,' he said.

'Nonsense,' said the Duke. 'You have no training. You're not a soldier. Leave it to those who are. Your use has been in giving us what may be useful intelligence. Now stay out of the way, please.'

'But, no, that wasn't . . . that's not the deal!' protested Will, the bitterness of betrayal choking him.

The Duke pinned him with a steely eye.

'The deal, young man, was we would help you to find your sister and free her. There was no talk of you coming along. The best way you can help us help you is to stay back here and let trained men, grown men, take it from here,' he said.

And with that he turned away and continued his briefing. Will felt more frustrated than he'd ever felt in his life. A tiny part of him was sort of relieved that he wasn't going to have to fight more dragons, but he knew that was the scared part of him, and the need to get Jo back was much bigger than that. He couldn't just stay behind. But nobody wanted to hear him.

He looked down at Tragedy, who just shrugged.

'Best do as he says,' the small boy muttered uncomfortably.

Will felt utterly alone, as nastily alone as you can only really be in a large crowd that's ignoring you. All he wanted, all he felt he needed, was for just one person to back him up. But Tragedy was avoiding his eyes and the Georges had disappeared into the group surrounding the Duke.

'No,' said Will. 'No.'

'Quite right,' said a woman's voice that he heard in the same instant he felt the wind from the downbeat of a pair of wings landing behind him. He turned and saw the Finsbury Victory standing behind him. She smiled grimly and put a hand on his shoulder.

It may have been a grim smile, but Will felt it light him up like sunshine.

'You came,' he said.

'I said I'd try,' she agreed. 'Now let's get these men organized!'

She stuck two fingers in her mouth, and let rip a loud and most unladylike whistle that cut through the hubbub like an axe.

The Duke looked up and as he stared at her all the other soldiers followed his gaze.

'You have something to say, ma'am?' he said.

'I do. I was telling the boy he is right,' she said. 'And now I'm telling you.'

'And what are you telling, ma'am?' he said, dangerously polite.

'I'm telling him he is right to want to go with your scouting party. How else can they identify his sister from the multitude of people no doubt frozen inside the museum? He'll definitely have to go along, if only so you can keep your word to him.'

'He's just a boy,' said the Duke. 'This is man's business.'

'He killed a dragon,' said Victory. 'I saw it. If you don't believe me, it's stuck to the railings at Coram's Fields. Show him the shield, boy.'

Will raised the dragon's shield. The soldiers muttered amongst themselves. It was a rather impressed kind of muttering.

The Duke met her eyes.

'Well,' he said. 'I'd be a rotten kind of general if

I spent my time arguing against victory I suppose. Very well. The boy goes too.'

Will had that conflicted, sick feeling in the pit of his stomach again. He was elated and terrified at the same time. In fact now he'd won the argument, that tiny scared part of his brain seemed to be expanding at breakneck speed. His mouth was dry and his heart was thumping like a bass drum. He had the nasty thought that whereas these spits could revive if they were hurt and put back on their plinths by midnight, he had no option to play again.

He couldn't revive.

For them, if things went wrong, it would just be a fight.

That was why they were so cheerful.

For him it would be Game Over.

And no reboot.

19

The Raid

The soldiers who were chosen for what the Duke called 'the scouting patrol' came together through the milling crowd of other disappointed statues and began to organize themselves. Will felt dwarfed by them as they clustered around. It seemed there were soldiers from all periods in Britain's history, from sword-bearing knights to men in tin hats and serious-looking rifles.

A World War One officer carrying a raincoat untangled himself from a binocular case and handed the coat to a tough-looking companion with a groundsheet worn over his uniform like a cape.

'Hold these for me 'til we get back will you, Gunner?' he said. 'Don't think it's going to rain . . .'

The Gunner took them and winked at Will.

'Just a bleeding valet, me,' he said.

The Officer turned and shook Will's hand.

'Don't worry young shaver,' he grinned. 'Stick close

and you'll be fine. We've got heavy cavalry and air support.'

He pointed at two full-sized knights with lances, introduced as more St Georges, one from Regent's Park, the other from somewhere called Dorset Rise.

'And you know this fellow, I gather,' said the Officer, pointing downwards.

'Hello old thing,' said one of the small Georges looking back at him. 'Fancy meeting you here. Welcome to the bunfight and all that rot.'

'And this is the Pilot. He'll be watching over us,' continued The Officer.

Will saw a flyer in a World War Two flying helmet and a life jacket. His arms were attached to wide spreading wings that hung over them, blotting out the view of the watery church roof above them.

'What ho!' said the Pilot. 'Don't worry. I'll just stooge up over the museum roof and have a bit of a shufty. Be a piece of cake.'

Will definitely wished people would stop talking about cakes and bunfights because it reminded him of how hungry he was, but most of all he wanted them to stop telling him not to worry, because all that did was remind him of the very many things he should be worrying about.

He was still thinking this and feeling even more starving a quarter of an hour later, as he found himself moving through the backstreets of Bloomsbury at the centre of a tight squad of soldiers who had closed round them like well-armed brick.

One of the St Georges rode ahead, and the other bought up the rear.

So far the toughest opponent they had faced was Little Tragedy who had to be forcibly restrained by The Gunner to prevent him joining the raiding party. Victory had stayed with him, a firm hand on his other shoulder as she waved Will off.

'Thank you,' he said. 'For coming back and backing me up . . .'

She nodded.

'Good luck, boy.'

Her face was serious. If she'd smiled, even just a fraction, he'd have thought 'good luck' was just a pleasantry, like 'have a nice day!' or 'see ya!'. Because there was no smile with it, he had the strong and unwelcome sense that she felt he was going to need luck to get out of this in one piece. He raised his hand in a sketchy farewell and turned away with the rest of the patrol.

No one talked. They communicated by hand signals

as they filtered through the stuck traffic and frozen people as if they were just inanimate obstacles in a normal landscape, like rocks and trees.

Will tried to keep his spirits up by remembering the encouraging words the Duke had sent him off with.

'Take heart young Mr Will,' he'd said. 'This London is the ancient capital of a very stubborn, terrier-like nation. As you see if you look around you, it is positively bulging with statues glorifying its many warriors. If there is something attacking it, it will find a rather formidable army ready to jump on its neck, magic or no magic. We do not lack reinforcements.'

This had lifted his spirits a little, and being at the centre of this warlike group certainly felt better than running through the streets with nothing but the heavy shield to protect him. Though as he thought that, he realized he was finding the shield easier to carry. Maybe he was getting used to it.

A soldier in a grenadier's bearskin carrying a long rifle stopped and raised a hand, signalling a halt. Everyone went still.

The Grenadier crept back to the Officer and spoke quietly into his ear, pointing round the corner for emphasis. The Officer turned to Will and crouched down so he was eye-to-eye.

'He says the yard in front of the museum is empty of everything except frozen people, but the doors are wide open. Anything could be watching from within though . . .'

He took his binoculars out of their case.

'I'm going for a closer look. Stay put.' He turned and gave the Pilot a thumbs up. Without another word, the Pilot had spread his wings and lifted into the night sky.

The Officer ran low across the street and took up position against the outer wall of the museum front yard. He aimed his binoculars between the railings and trained them on the building.

After a couple of minutes he turned and ran back at a crouch. The Pilot landed softly beside him.

'Right,' he said to Will as much as the Officer. 'Debrief. Your sister, same colour hair as you, blue T-shirt, hooded sweater, red gym shoes?'

Will nodded, his heart racing.

'There's a hole in the dome,' said the Pilot. 'Something broke a pane of glass. I had a dekko inside. She was pretty easy to spot actually. The only one of the frozen people in the Great Court who was looking terrified, and certainly the only one being guarded by a big beetle job like the one you're wearing.'

'A scarab?' said Will.

'Big as a sofa. Ugly thing. Walking round her in circles. Quite close to the front entrance actually. Some other kind of chanting going on, sounds like people gargling in the bath, but probably magic. Can see strange blue lights from Egyptian Gallery. So your hunch was good.'

The Officer handed Will the binoculars.

'Come on,' he said, 'keep low and have a look.'

He pointed at a messenger cyclist who was standing on the pavement, stuck in the act of pouring water from a bottle down his throat, his bike leaning against the outer wall.

'Go by the bicyclist and you'll have a good angle to see some of the inside through the open door.'

Will ran with the Grenadier across the road and knelt by the bicycle. He put the binoculars to his eyes and peered inside the door of the museum, fifty metres away. He could see shapes, backlit by a strange blue light.

He couldn't see Jo though.

And then his heart jumped as the lights shifted a bit, and just for a second he saw what was unmistakably the side of her head.

'That's her,' he said excitedly.

The other soldiers had gathered behind the wall beside him and leant in for a quick conference.

'Right,' said the Pilot. 'If she's close enough to see, she's close enough to snatch. In, out, fast and hard, the Georges in first, heavy armour at speed, supported in force by—'

'No,' said the Officer. 'I'm sorry, but no. We have to report back. I don't know what the blue lights are, but they're not good.'

He did look truly sorry.

'But,' said Will in disbelief. 'But you all promised . . .'

'We'll still get her back all right,' said the Officer. 'Just not right now. This is too big a discovery. Wiser heads need to think about this. It's about all London, all the other Regulars too you know. Not just your sister. But we will be back for her.'

There was a cough from waist level. Everyone looked down. The two small Georges stood there with their hands bobbing in the air, like schoolboys trying to get the teachers attention.

'Er. Sorry, old fruit . . . I mean Sir, but how d'you know doors'll be open?' said the first George, smiling up at the Officer. 'When you come back?'

The other George nodded his head.

'George here makes a good point, old man,' he said. 'You can't be sure, can you?'

'It's not about being sure. It's about making a best guess in a bad situation. And tactically, this is it,' said the Officer. 'Sorry.'

Will felt this was an argument he was going to lose. He could see the shape of it, the sense of it. He knew how grown-ups could talk their way round so that whatever they wanted to do was right.

'Seriously Will,' said the Officer. 'I am sorry. But be patient. Think about it. We can't just run in and be fast enough to expect whatever's in there to just . . .'

'I'm not going to run,' snapped Will. The George was right.

That open door was now.

'Now' was all he could control.

Next time it could be closed and barred and he would not be able to see Jo, not then, maybe never.

And that was not acceptable.

He slung the shield over his back like a messenger bag, and took the bicycle handles out of the cyclist's unresisting hands.

'Wait,' said the Officer. 'That's an order.'

Will threw his leg over the crossbar and was about to start pedalling when the small George leapt in front of him with his lance.

'Hold on!' he said.

'Don't try to stop me,' Will gritted through clenched teeth.

'Who's trying to stop you, you fathead?' said the George. 'Give me a leg up, there's a good chap.'

'You two! Stop right there,' said the Officer. 'That's an order!'

'Sorry sir,' grinned the small knight as he climbed up onto the handlebars in front of George. 'Not an actual soldier. Am a George. Meant to be a saint thingy. Answer to a higher authority and all that . . .'

And before anyone could grab him, before he could have a second thought, Will focused all his concentration on his legs and the image of Jo's profile he had glimpsed through the open door.

He worked his aching leg muscles up and down faster than he had ever done before in his life.

The bicycle accelerated through the yard towards the shallow steps. The George got his lance sorted out and pointed it ahead of them, so that by the time George hit the wheelchair ramp they were at full ramming speed and ready for action.

He heard the Officer shouting orders behind him, but didn't turn to see what was happening. He heard hoof beats break into a gallop as the full-size Georges spurred their mounts forward.

What he didn't see was two dragons erupting from where they'd been lying hidden and racing to meet them. He was going so fast and making such a headlong assault that he had actually surprised the ambush that Bast had set by leaving Jo in plain sight.

Sometimes fortune favours the brave; sometimes it favours the foolhardy.

The bike went airborne from the top of the disabled ramp and headed through the doorway half a metre off the ground.

He heard the George on the handlebars laughing exultantly . . .

. . . and then one of the lion-women appeared out of nowhere blocking their way and it suddenly looked like the game was over before it had really begun. He began to squeeze the brakes . . .

. . . but then there was the sound of gunfire from behind him and he felt a round smacking past his ear.

The lion-woman was knocked backwards, out of their way.

He took his hand off the brake lever and pedalled harder.

Will saw Jo, penned behind a slab of reception

desk, and steered for her. Only then did he hit the brakes and jump off. The George leapt for the top of the desk and skidded to a halt.

Will scrabbled in his pocket and felt for Jo's bracelet. He gripped her hand, a nasty shiver of fear running through him as he noted how cold and lifeless it was. It wasn't at all like the strangely comforting warmth they'd both felt from their frozen mother. That seemed like aeons ago. Hard to believe it had really been just a few hours earlier.

His heart was pounding as he got the bracelet out of his pocket. All his vision seemed to tunnel down into a narrow cone centred on Jo's face, the face he knew so well, the one that annoyed him more than any other, that made him laugh more than any other, the one that – more than any other – felt like home, the terrible face that now looked so horribly unmoving and dead and frightened. He was terrified himself, scared that Jo's face wouldn't come back to life when he put the bracelet on, petrified that he had no idea what he'd do then, and at the same time exultant and disbelieving that his mad bicycle dash had worked, that he just maybe was about to succeed . . .

He squashed the fear with that jubilant thought. The Duke was wrong. He'd done it.

'Yes!' he said, reaching out with the scarab.

'NO!'

The voice boomed and yowled around the huge internal courtyard as the cat Bast leapt at him, hitting him with such force that he dropped the bracelet which skittered away across the floor into the shadows.

It was the dragon's shield that saved him.

As he reflexively twisted away from the attacking cat, the heavy metal strapped diagonally across his back like a messenger bag shifted and slipped round his shoulder, the great weight giving it such momentum that the edge of the shield caught the cat in the side of the skull just below the earring. Metal clanged on metal and the cat staggered sideways, stunned.

Will ducked his head and shucked out of the strap which was about to entangle him, and in the short moment it took the cat to shake and clear its own head, got his arm through the strap and held it properly, so that when the cat leapt back into the attack he was able to protect himself.

Sparks flew as Bast slashed scimitar-sharp claws across the front of the shield, claws that Will knew would have taken his face off if he hadn't been on the right side of the protective metal.

The cat leapt again and Will parried, matching

speed for speed.

Even as he did so he marvelled at his reflexes.

He was moving fast, almost as if he knew which way the cat would attack, almost as if he wasn't having to think – and then he realized that he *wasn't* thinking. The shield was helping. The shield was thinking for him, making him stronger, quicker . . . maybe even more dangerous.

The cat snarled and sprang at him again, the gold in its ears and nose glinting as it did something totally impossible and changed direction in mid-air, wrong-footing him . . . but even then, even though it was fast and sneaky and defied the laws of physics in the way it moved, Will and the shield were faster. The shield was like a power-up, like an added ability.

He swatted the airborne cat in a powerful backhand that thwacked it into the marble desk with a resounding crash.

Will's eyes scoured the shadowy floor looking for the bracelet.

The cat got to its feet, but did not return to the attack.

Instead it turned towards Jo.

'SAY GOODBYE TO YOUR SISTER,' it spat.

Will's guts turned to ice water.

The cat sprang towards Jo.

Will dived despairingly for the cat, chopping the edge of the shield down, trying to block it.

The cat was too fast. Will missed it.

But the shield smacked into the ground and trapped its tail.

There was an undignified YERK sound as the mighty Bast was pulled up short, and then Will, remembering what Tragedy had told him about the fate of the other cat, Hodge, grabbed the tail in his right hand and spun.

He spun round one and a half times, the weight of the shield on his outflung left arm acting as a counterweight to the unexpectedly heavy cat howling in fury as centrifugal force whirled it out at the very end of its tail, like a hammer-throw in the Olympics.

'This is for The Fusilier!' he grunted. 'And this is for attacking my sister!'

And then Will let go with a mighty heave that wrenched all his muscles, and the cat sailed across the shadowy courtyard and slammed into the top of a forty-foot redwood tree-trunk carved into a totem-pole with such force that one of the cat's flailing claws accidentally chunked into the wood, leaving it to hang there lifelessly suspended above the floor far below.

'Here!' shouted a voice from behind him. 'Catch!'

He turned to see the George on the reception desk leaning down and fishing something off the floor with the tip of his lance. It was the bracelet. He flicked it across to Will who caught it on reflex.

'Get a bend on!' said the George. 'We should be going!'

Will grabbed Jo's outflung, frozen hand and slammed the scarab into it. She jerked as if he'd given her an electric shock, and gasped at him. He felt a jolt of unexpected, answering happiness as he saw the life flood back into life.

'Will!' she cried.

He grinned and closed her fist over the scarab.

'Don't let go of that' he shouted. 'Whatever you do, keep hold and . . .'

He looked round. He had intended to cycle straight out of there, but hadn't thought how hard it would be to get her on board quick enough.

'Just RUN!' he yelled and yanked her towards the door.

The giant scarab erupted out of the shadows in front of them and blocked their way. It was bigger and much nastier than a sofa, and its wings unfolded into whirring angry half discs of sharp black stone.

Will froze, looking for a better direction to escape to.

There was an open door to an inner gallery, a gallery with blue light and dark shadows bouncing round it. He was about to pull her in that direction when the lion-women came out of it at speed. One with a stick snarled and headed for them, the others ran for the front door.

Something howled between Jo and Will, and hit the scarab like a battering ram, knocking it onto its back, where it spun, legs angrily flailing, chittering as it tried to get itself the right way up.

Filax barked and jumped sideways, putting himself between Jo and the charging lion-woman.

'Good dog!' shouted the George, and leapt off the reception desk to land right between the scarab's legs, pinning it to the floor with his long lance.

The lion-woman slashed her weapon at Filax at the same time that he leapt for her.

There was a sickening thwack of stone on stone, and then they fell together into a yowling snarling ball of fury as each tried to rip out the other's throat.

'KILL THEM! KILL THEM ALL!!' boomed a voice from the top of the totem pole. Bast had regained consciousness and was struggling to free her claw from the dense wood, convulsively twisting in rage as she did so, wholly unconcerned about the long drop beneath her.

'Run boy!' shouted the George.

Will grabbed Jo and they sprinted for the door.

Two lion-women were pushing the tall metal doors closed. Freedom was just a few paces away, but the gap to it was closing fast.

They weren't going to make it.

The narrow slit suddenly disappeared as someone leapt into it.

The Officer braced a hand on either door and pushed back against the lion-women.

'Come on then!' he shouted. 'Get a bend on!'

The grenadier jumped in behind him and threw his weight against the doors.

One of the lion-women looked round the edge of the door and snarled.

'Soldiers!' she roared. 'Soldier statues!'

Will saw the door begin to close again.

The Officer waited until Will was right on him, then he let go of the door, grabbed Jo and threw himself backwards. The doors began to slam, but Will's shield jammed the gap open. The strap parted and he tumbled out onto the steps.

Looking back inside the museum he saw the blue lights begin to flicker faster and faster and heard a voice that appeared to come from everywhere roar in anger as the whole building seemed to vibrate into a blur.

'ALL WHO BEAR ARMS AGAINST US, TREMBLE AND BOW DOWN! ALL SOLDIERS AND WEAPON BEARERS, HEAR THE WORD OF MIGHTY BAST THE HUNTRESS!'

The shield holding the door open began to buckle under the pressure of the force being exerted on it, and then two things happened at once: it flexed and spanged out, flying over Jo's and Will's heads, and as the door slammed shut with a noise like the crack of doom itself, the dog Filax hurtled out of it.

Will stared at the closed doors and realized what it meant.

'George!' he cried. 'The George is stuck in there—'

'No I'm bally well not' said a voice.

He looked down to see the knight was holding on to the shaggy mane of the dog, which he had ridden to safety.

Will's heart leaped with elation. Everything was going to be all right.

Even Jo's hand, which seemed to be clutching his

212

own, was reassuringly warm.

He grinned at her. He didn't have the words. She grinned right back at him.

Epilogue

There was still some struggling and movement going on outside as they hurried back toward the road. The small knight riding the large dog patted its side and grinned up at them.

'Always wanted a horse of my own,' he said. 'But I think this plucky mutt is rather better. What I like about this fell—'

Will was about to introduce Jo when the bad thing happened, and the happy ending changed into something else entirely.

'BE STILL!' roared the voice from inside the museum.

The walls flexed with a silent detonation, and a ring of blue radiated out across the ground. As the thin blue curve that marked the blast radius passed over them, each of the soldier statues froze in whatever position they were in.

The George never got to finish what he was saying

about the dog, The Officer was stuck with his mouth open, the two Georges who Will now saw had been detained outside the museum by a pair of dragons, stopped dead, and one by one the soldiers stopped moving.

'Will?' said Jo. She was groggy, like someone who has been asleep. 'Will, what's that?'

There was a terrible crash as something fell out of the night sky and bounced off the roof of the museum.

It was the Pilot. Stiff as a bar of iron.

The only thing that moved was a small bronze boy who had obviously escaped the Gunner's custody, and who ran over and dragged Jo and Will into motion, yanking them out of their shock and leading them away from the museum and the still ominous vibration within.

'Come on! We got to get out of here,' he said. 'It's all gone for a ball of chalk!'

'Will!' said Jo. 'Really. What's happening?'

Will couldn't speak. He was staring at all the terrible frozen soldiers. The Duke's words about London being safe because it had so many military statues rang hollowly in his ears.

'He saved you,' said Tragedy.

'Of course he did,' she said, as if it was the most

215

natural thing in the world. 'He's my brother. And he's not a coward, even if he says he is.'

Will stopped, stunned.

'You heard . . . ?'

'. . . the last thing you said to me before I was taken here? Yes I heard that and no: you're not a coward, stupid. Annoying, yes. A coward, no.'

She might as well have suckerpunched him.

'But I didn't jump Jo, when you thought I'd jumped like you did, I hadn't . . .' he said.

'I know' she said.

He stared at her.

'Doofus. I saw you! You lowered yourself halfway and jumped the rest. I was watching from the bushes before you came and found me with your big dare.'

'You never said . . .' he began.

'You said quite enough,' she laughed.

'When?' he said. 'When did I say anything? I didn't! I should have but I didn't.'

She shook her head in disbelief.

'When you jumped down after me? When you tried to help me stand up, before we realized how bad my leg was and I fainted, you were gabbling all about it, saying sorry and explaining . . .'

She trailed off.

'You don't remember?'

He remembered gabbling in terror, he remembered the panic. But he had no clue what he'd said.

'I told you?' he asked. 'But why, why didn't you tell me I'd told you?'

'I thought we'd just sort of silently agreed not to talk about it,' she shrugged. 'Will. You double-doofus! Is this what you've been sulking about all year?'

He didn't know what to say. His head was buzzing with a heady cocktail of relief, adrenaline and deep fear of whatever was going on behind them in the museum. But most of all it was the relief of Jo looking normally at him. He was about to say so when Tragedy hopped between them.

'I don't want to interrupt all this nice chat, but in case you hadn't noticed, all the soldiers is froze stiff as the Regulars. Never seen nothing like it.'

His words reminded Will of something, a thought he'd pushed to the back of his mind ever since he had touched the roller-skating girl back in the supermarket. He stopped and reached out to touch the hand of a woman frozen in the act of opening an umbrella. She was not just cool. She was cold. An answering chill went through him. She was almost frozen in more ways than one.

217

'The people are losing their heat,' he said. 'Feel. This woman's hands are freezing . . .'

Jo reached over. Touched the hand. Then the face. Then she touched the face of a street-sweeper emptying a bin beside her.

'They're all going to be frozen in more ways than one if they keep on like this,' she said, her voice rising. 'It's not over then Will, is it? We can't just . . . wake up now, can we?'

'No,' said Will tearing his eyes from the unmoving soldiers as they ducked into a narrow street and picked up speed.

'No. I don't think we can. We got you back – but I think I broke everything else. And I think we need to stop this before everyone gets too cold ever to wake again.'

He saw her suck it up in one long breath.

'OK,' she said. 'Fine. That's what we do then.'

And then they pounded down the road for a long time, turning right and left as Tragedy led them, in silence.

After a bit Jo stopped hobbling at speed and slowed. And after a shorter bit she stopped completely and rubbed her leg.

There was a noise behind them. Will instinctively

stepped protectively in front of Jo as the creature hurtled round the corner.

It was Filax.

He was carrying something.

He dropped it at Will's feet and looked expectantly at them.

It was the bent Dragon Shield.

Jo bent and ruffled the dog's ears. Its tail thumped happily on the ground. She met Will's eyes.

'Sorry,' she said.

'Me too,' said Will. 'We'll get you a bike or something. Maybe find another chair.'

'So this isn't the end,' she said looking at him, clear-eyed for the first time since he'd rescued her.

'No,' he said. 'I think it's worse than that. I think it's just begun.'

She looked over at Little Tragedy. He smiled at her. She nodded and looked back at Will.

'At least we're together,' she said. 'However bad things are going to get, that's a good start.'

'Yeah,' he said, picking up the shield and patting the dog. 'Yeah. That's good.'

And for now, just for now, it was.

. . . to be continued.

If you liked *Dragon Shield*, then you'll love *Stoneheart*! Set in the same world, George finds himself plunged into a world he doesn't understand after he breaks a carving in the Natural History Museum . . . Read on for a sample . . .

1

BELLY OF THE WHALE
AND THE MONKEY'S TEETH

George never spent any time wondering why he wanted
to belong. He just did. Things were like that. You were
in or you were out, and in was a lot safer. It wasn't the
sort of thing you questioned. It was just there.

On the class trip before this one they'd been to the
War Museum and learned all about trench warfare.
George had thought that's what life felt like: just
keeping your head below the parapet so you wouldn't
get hit.

Of course that was last year, in the past, like all the
other things about being a kid. He still thought about
them sometimes. He still remembered what being a
kid was like. But he was over that. He was twelve. Real
Twelve, not 'Only Twelve', as his father had called it
the last time they'd spoken. He knew *his* twelve wasn't
anything like his dad's because he'd seen pictures of

his dad as a kid looking clueless and speccy and fat, all of which – in George's twelve-year-old trench – would be the equivalent of sitting on top of the parapet with a big round target painted on your head yelling, 'Cooee, over here'.

George could remember talking and laughing about stuff like that with his dad, before his dad moved out and there was too much talking altogether.

He didn't say much at home any more. His mother complained about it, usually to him, but sometimes to other people late at night on the phone when she thought he was asleep. Somewhere inside it hurt when he heard her say that – not as much as when she said he used to have such a lovely smile – but nearly.

And nowhere near as much as never being able to say anything to his dad ever again.

The thing was he wasn't *not* saying anything on purpose. It was something that seemed to have just happened, like his baby teeth falling out, or getting taller. Mind you, he wasn't getting taller as fast as he would have liked, and right now that was part of the problem.

He was average height for his age, maybe even a bit more – but somehow he *felt* shorter, the same way he sometimes felt older than he was. Or maybe it wasn't exactly older, just a bit more worn and rumpled than his classmates – rather like his clothes. His clothes were all thrown in the same washing machine, colours and whites together, and though his mother said it made no difference, it did. It made everything pale and grey and washed out, and that's exactly what George felt like most of the time.

It was certainly what he felt like today, and not being able to see properly was making him feel more insignificant than usual; all he could make out was the whale's belly and the back of his classmates' heads as they clustered round a museum guide showing them something interesting. George tried to push forward, but all he got was an elbow in his ribs. He sidled round the pack and tried to get another view, careful not to push anyone.

He found a place where he could nearly hear and edged closer, peering through the thin gap between a circular stand full of pamphlets and a boy about four inches taller than him. As he rattled the stand with his shoulder and reached to steady it, the boy turned and registered him.

George found himself smiling at him on reflex. The boy didn't return fire on the smile. He just looked away without comment. George wasn't too worried about being blanked. In fact he was relieved. The boy was the name-maker, the one with the gift for finding the cruellest nicknames for his peers, then making them stick. He'd almost been a friend of George's when they'd all been new together, but finding his gift had given him a kind of easy invulnerability, a power that meant he didn't have to have friends any more, only followers. That's what made him dangerous.

The boy turned back round. This time he spoke. 'Something I can help you with?'

George froze. Then tried to hide the freeze with another smile and a shrug. 'No. Uh. Just getting a better—'

'Don't stand behind me.'

The boy turned away. But several others had seen, and in their eyes George saw something he recognized. Not interest, certainly not sympathy, not even much dislike. Just a pale gratitude that they weren't the target this time.

So George swallowed and stayed where he was. He knew enough not to be seen being pushed around. He knew once you did that you were sunk. He knew there was a level below which you couldn't afford to sink, because once you were down there, there was no ladder back up. Once you were in that pit, you were fair game for everyone, and everyone unloaded on you.

So he looked down at the square of marble he stood on and decided he'd stick to it. There were teachers present, anyway. What's the worst that could happen?

The boy calmly reached backwards and toppled the stand, right into George. He stepped back, but there wasn't enough room, so he batted at the metal column with his hands to protect himself. It hit the floor with a loud metallic crash, spilling pamphlets all across the tiling around George.

The room went suddenly very quiet. Faces turned. The boy turned with them, innocent-looking amazement quickly morphing into shocked surprise.

'Chrissakes, Chapman!'

The cluster of boys around him dissolved into hooting anarchy, and the three adults, two teachers and a guide, were left looking for the culprit. And with everyone else doubled up and pointing, there he was, head above the parapet, feet bogged down in a landslide of bright-coloured paper booklets.

Mr Killingbeck fixed him with a sniper's eye, crooked a bony trigger finger at him and fired a one-word bullet.

'Chapman.'

George felt his face reddening. Killingbeck snapped his fingers at the other boys.

'The rest of you clear Chapman's mess up! You – follow me.'

George walked after him as he stepped away from the mob.

He followed him out of the whale room back into the central hall of the Natural History Museum. Mr Killingbeck stopped in the middle of the room beneath the dinosaur skeleton and beckoned him closer.

George had enough experience of Mr Killingbeck to know not to start what was coming. So he just waited. The man's mouth worked slowly. He always worked his mouth as if everything that he said tasted bad, and had to be spat out before it caused him more pain and discomfort.

'Mmm, tell me, were you trying to be rude, Chapman, or does it just come naturally?'

'It wasn't me, sir.'

'Who was it then?'

There was no answer to that. No answer George could give. He knew it. Killingbeck knew it. So he didn't say anything.

'Moral cowardice and dumb insolence. Neither very

appealing, Chapman. Neither what you were sent here to learn, are they?'

George wondered what planet Killingbeck was on. Planet 1970-something probably. Not a planet where George could breathe. He began to get choked up. His face began a slow burn that he could feel without seeing.

'That was unforgivable, boy. You behaved like something wholly uncivilized. Like that ape over there.'

The bony finger jabbed at a monkey in a glass cage, baring its teeth in the grimace that would be the last message it ever sent to the world. George knew what it felt like.

'You're uncivilized, Chapman. What are you?'

George just looked at the monkey, thinking how strong and frightening its teeth looked. More like fangs really.

Killingbeck worked his mouth.

George found the blob of Plasticene in his pocket and began kneading it with his fingers. It still had the knobbly contours of a face he'd made on the bus.

'I think it's worth something more than sullen silence, Chapman. I think it's worth an apology for a start.'

George's thumb coasted over the open mouth in the Plasticene face and wedged it a bit wider.

'Get your hands out of your pockets.'

George smashed the nose on the Plasticene and pulled his hand out of his pocket.

'You're going to say sorry if you have to stand there all day. Do you understand?'

George worked the Plasticene in his fist.

'Or you can tell me who you say did it. Do you understand?'

George understood. There was a rock. There was a hard place. And then there was him, jammed up between the two. He couldn't grass on another boy, even a bully, because grassing would drop him into a place so low in the eyes of the other boys that not only was there no ladder back up, but there was no floor either. Grass someone up, and the rest of your life would be spent in free-fall down a pit that just got deeper and darker and never stopped.

That was the rock.

That was simple.

The hard place was less simple, maybe because it was so big, so immovable.

The hard place was everything else.

The hard place was his life.

The hard place was everything that led to this moment.

And the moment was clamping round him and giving him nowhere to run.

'Chapman?' Killingbeck's finger tapped impatiently on the side crease of his trousers.

George looked at the monkey's fangs. How easily they'd snap through that impatient stick of flesh and brittle bone. He'd like to have those teeth in his head. He'd like to bite that finger off and spit it back at Killingbeck. He'd like it so much that he could feel the crunch and crack and almost taste the blood. The feeling was so immediate, so nearly real that he was suddenly frightened by it as it hung black and treacly in his mind. He'd *never* had a thought like that. The shock made him reel inside and forget he wasn't speaking.

'Sir?'

'Well?' Killingbeck's voice jerked him back into the now, back between the rock and the hard place. He didn't know what he was going to do. But he suddenly knew from the prickling in his eyes that there was one treacherous possibility.

George was not going to cry. And knowing what he *wasn't* going to do suddenly made it all clear. He knew what to do, what to say. And he knew to say it very slowly, very calmly so as not to let the thing rising in his throat choke him.

'I understand that's what you think I should do, sir.'

Killingbeck looked at him with the surprise of a hungry man whose dinner just bit back. His mouth stopped chewing at the next thing he was going to say.

'I just don't agree with it.'

The pupils in Killingbeck's eyes irissed down to the size of full-stops.

George knew he'd made a mistake. He knew, with a sudden flash of intimacy which scared him more than the finger-biting image, that Killingbeck wanted to hurt him. He could feel the itch in the man's hand as the bony fingers blunted into a fist.

'Well. Well, well, well. That's fine.' Killingbeck closed his eyes and ran his free hand through the thick grey hair that curled back round his skull, as if he was trying to massage the very thought of George out of his head. 'You'll stay here until you decide to apologize. If you haven't done so by the time we leave, you will be in more trouble than you can imagine. You will stand straight, you will not sit down, you will not put your hands in your pockets, you will not chew at sweets, you will not move from this spot. The museum guards will not let you out unless you are with the rest of the party. We will pick you up in an hour and a half and you will apologize then, in front of everyone. Do you understand *that*?'

His eyes snapped open. George didn't flinch. 'Yes.'

Killingbeck 180'd and strode off after the rest of the class.

George listened to the click of his heels across the stone floor.

Then he put his hands in his pockets. Then he sat down on a bench. Then he put a piece of chewing gum in his mouth.

And then he got up, walked to the door and out into the drizzle that was soaking the steps in front of the museum.

The guards didn't give him a second look.